METAMORPHOSIS

A Short Story Collection

By

Rebecca S Meadows

METAMORPHOSIS - A Short Story Collection

ISBN: 978-1-7349947-3-5 (Paperback)
ISBN: 978-1-7349947-6-6 (Ebook)

Published by BLUE BUTTERFLY ENTERPRISES, LLC

TABLE OF CONTENTS

GROWING HAIR ON YOUR CHEST 1

Foreword 3

The Mind's Battle vs. God's Faithful Promise 5

Faith Is the Answer 6

Reach Out to God in Childlike Faith 7

Salvation and Survival 7

THE TRIALS of TRACEY JONES 9

Chapters 1–13. 11-44

Epilogue. 45

SO, WHAT NOW?. 47

Chapters 1–8 49-64

Epilogue. 65

SAVING BETH'S BABY. 67

Chapters 1–31. 69-134

Afterword 136

GRETCH THE WRETCH 137

Chapters 1–12. 139-179

Afterword 181

MY PREMONITION **183**

Chapters 1–5 185-194

Afterword 194

About the Author 195

GROWING
HAIR ON YOUR CHEST

FOREWORD

A Brutal Word from Blind Becca

I'll be brief. I just want to share a secret with you.

Are you ready? It's a doozie.

You have the power to change your own life. God put the power right inside you when He created you.

This is true no matter what you've been told by the people who surround you. It is true regardless of what your current circumstances are.

As long as you are breathing; you have the potential to accomplish extraordinary things in this world.

This is particularly true if you are blessed enough to live in the United States of America.

There you have it; you've been told the naked truth. You no longer have any excuse for sitting around being a pain in everyone's ass. Get off your butt and go do something constructive with your life.

I get so tired of listening to people complaining about their situations. It's always easy to find someone who's experiencing worse circumstances than you. So suck it up buttercup! I don't want to hear it anymore.

THE MIND'S BATTLE VS.
GOD'S FAITHFUL PROMISE

Change the message your mind's receiving and you can change your world forever. I know this is the ultimate ticket. This is how I finally beat them all.

From the moment I woke up at the age of twelve years old, I had doctors, nurses, orderlies, therapists, counselors, attorneys, teachers, all my peers, my own mother and total strangers lying to me. And each one of them was speaking from their narrow perspective. I was forced to argue with them all for years.

Imagine what it did for my case the day I realized I was literally the only person in the world who could possibly have any idea of what was really going on? They were the ones who had told me how unique my situation was. I was the only person who had experienced such a devastating event and survived to tell and go public with it. What made them think they could possibly know more about what was going on inside me than I did?

The day I embraced this logic; I knew I would ultimately outsmart them.

God gave me what I needed from the very beginning. Learning to balance that child-like faith against the terrifying reality that had engulfed my world became my tallest order. This was the beginning of my quest to find and plant my own mustard seed.

I set about holding God to His word from the very beginning. Back then, I had the rest of my life to spend waiting on the fulfillment of His promises.

Thank goodness I figured out how to jumpstart the manifestation of His miracles in my everyday life.

Faith is the Answer

Did I believe or didn't I? I had to decide once and for all where I stood on this eternal question when I was just twelve years old.

If the doctors were correct; I might as well just have kissed my ass goodbye.

On the other hand, God had said something completely different long ago . . . He promised He would be faithful to those who have faith in Him.

I had always known what His Word professed. Dare I put Him to the test now?

I realized I had no other option. I had to figure out how to walk by faith if I were ever going to claim His promised blessings. I knew I had only the rest of my life to accomplish this feat.

How does one do this? Walking by faith and manifesting the fulfillment of God's promises can be tricky. Your human nature keeps getting in the way.

I went back to the basics. I knew well what God's Word said; it was written on the walls of my heart when I was just a girl.

He commanded us to not judge. I had been judged and misjudged by most of the world since I first woke up. As a result, I learned how not to judge; for the most part.

He commanded to consider your neighbor's needs before yours.

While everyone around me was taking advantage of others (and especially me), I tried to be generous to all who came seeking goodwill from me.

God said we were to proclaim His miracles in the faces of nonbelievers even before they became a reality. I did this always to the doctors, lawyers and even to my own mother.

I spent so much time proclaiming His promised healing; they all thought I was nuts. I've been claiming God's healing for decades now.

Through all that turmoil; my mustard seed has been growing. God has been healing me according to the size of that faith all these years.

I don't want to toot my own horn. I've been winging it all the way. God blessed my efforts no matter how bumbling they became over the years.

Reach Out to God in Childlike Faith

Reaching out to God was a desperate attempt to save myself—both spiritually and physically.

I was so angry at Him, the doctor and the whole damn world for what had happened. I knew He was the responsible party from the very beginning.

He accepted all my anger and bitterness as I cried out to Him. With my childlike faith, I could almost feel His arms around me and hear His voice as my Heavenly Father comforted me all those decades ago.

It was only because of that childlike faith I was able to hold on through all the dark years that followed.

Salvation and Survival

The Bible says we were all created in the image of God. The ancient scriptures are full of references to the power and authority we have as His children.

Many people have forgotten His Words. As a result, they have lost hold of their inheritance. They have forgotten His promises, so they aren't walking in the manifestation of those vows.

They've become so scared of dying they don't even hear the blasphemous words coming out of their own mouths!

They've been denying God's existence their entire lives. Now, they ask why He hasn't just delivered their salvation to their inbox. They're kidding, right?

Well, enough fancy words. My point is straightforward and simple. It's time to get right with your Creator if you haven't already.

We're heading for very rough waters here, folks. Get ready to hold on tight. I'll try to help you navigate using what I've learned about surviving a socialist nightmare . . .

Always remember . . . God has the first and last word in your life; if you let Him.

God loves you and has a wonderful plan for your life if you will trust in Him.

You can do all things through Christ who strengthens you.

— The Measuring Life

THE TRIALS of TRACEY JONES

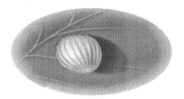

CHAPTER 1

Tracey Jones shivered as she walked up the snow-packed, crumbling concrete steps that led into the public school she had been attending most of her life. Her rural, farming community had experienced their first major snowstorm of the season over the weekend—on Halloween. No big shock. It seemed like it always snowed on Halloween.

Tracey had hated Halloween and everything that went with winter since she was suddenly blinded when she was just twelve years old. Life became extremely difficult after that. Dumping mountains of snow on top of her already difficult existence just seemed like a sick joke to Tracey. Why would a person want to dress up in plastic garments and go out into that crappy weather just to get some candy from strangers?

But her senseless parents made her do it . . . and that as a blind person. Without a cane. In the dark. And through the deep snow . . . It was all horrible, every minute of every single day. And Tracey just wanted it to be over.

Before the "accident" she was a straight-A student who read avidly and was active in the Girls Scouts, drill team and girls' basketball. She loved school and her dream was to be a teacher when she grew up.

She was the apple of her parents' eye; the oldest of four girls.

Then she woke up one day . . . literally and figuratively.

One day—it doesn't matter what day it was anymore—Tracey just woke up and found herself in this weird alternate reality.

Everyone suddenly treated her like she was only part of a person; and that part had somehow been irrevocably broken.

That was all anyone else cared about. What about the rest of Tracey? What about her hopes and dreams?

They didn't care. She wasn't supposed to dream—about anything. She was just supposed to accept what they told her and keep her mouth shut. What they had been telling her ever since she first woke up . . .

Now, here she was almost a third of the way through her senior year; her final year, in this hellhole.

Tracey couldn't wait to just get it over with.

She felt sure something was bound to change in her life after she managed to graduate from high school in the spring.

Honestly, she thought for a long time she may have stumbled into the legendary Twilight Zone. Who goes to sleep only to wake up later to be told a cockamamie story like this? Tracey was certain it must be some kind of weird dream . . . or nightmare, or something.

Tracey was finally forced to face the truth. And she was angry with God. Only He could have pulled this on her.

Tracey held Him personally responsible for this blunder in her life. It was He who claimed to have a "master plan" for her life. What was this?

Okay, okay. So, He did say there would be trials in life, but this was ridiculous.

Then Tracey remembered the scripture: " To whom much is given, much will be required." So, maybe to whom many trials are given; many blessings are poured out upon. Maybe God had a plan to bless her in a really big way later in life and this is why He was expecting so much suffering from her now.

This is the way Tracey's young mind reasoned it out anyway. Tracey looked at all her suffering as a sacrifice as unto the Lord. That's all she could do. She just about went mad if she allowed herself to look at the situation from any other perspective. Anything else would make all her suffering just one big loss. This mindset somehow got her all the way through junior high and high school. And this journey was incredibly rough.

All the mornings of getting out of bed and stepping into a lukewarm shower and shivering as she dried off after said shower. Then the trips up the stairs to seek out some kind of nourishment before leaving for school. Tracey's mother made it clear she was lucky she was allowed to eat with the others. The neglect and psychological abuse Tracey suffered at the hands of her own mother just made Tracey all the more determined to recover and outlive that bitch so she could get her revenge. What kind of woman makes her blind daughter hate life so much just because said child has been struck down?

And when Tracey finally made it to school every day; all the days she was in high school she couldn't read or write anything without a great deal of difficulty. This made it nearly impossible for her to learn.

She remembered all the tough days trudging through those hallways at school, feeling invisible. How was she supposed to make friends? She couldn't walk straight, and she saw everything twisted and at a distance.

She managed to fall down almost every single set of steps that were located throughout her sprawling school at one time or another over all these years. Except the stairs leading down from the stage in the pit in the center of the high school. Tracey was terrified of those stairs and the stage. She was certain she would break a leg or worse if she ever fell off of it. As a result, she avoided that area of the school as much as she could.

It was after she fell down the stairs leading to the basement one day that the light bulb finally went on in her scrambled brain. As Tracey lay there with her head rammed into the corner—where the concrete wall met the steps and the hard tile floor and her body crushed against the stairs behind her— she realized how close she came to smashing her already damaged brain against that cinder block wall. Her parents must want her dead. Why else would they send her to school every day in these conditions without a cane? And then there were all the times she nearly froze to death when she got lost out in the snow-covered streets. She didn't only get lost after dusk but in broad daylight as well. The glare of the sunshine as it hit her in the face when it bounced back from the white snow just blinded her even more. It was ridiculous!

Her parents obviously wanted her to die. Why else were they robbing her of a decent education and any hope at all?

Well, Tracey had shown them. She survived. Eventually, she even thrived . . . She didn't give in to suicide either. She had always known that was the coward's way out of any situation. And yes, she may be a lot of things, but a coward was not one of them.

She didn't allow her body to just stop and die either. She managed to narrowly avoid a myriad of "accidents" that could have seriously maimed or even killed her over the years.

She used her scrambled brain as much as she could to exercise it and make it work better. She knew they couldn't stop her from what she was doing. They were all so busy scheming about how they would get their hands on her money eventually—if she lost. She just kept pushing herself to keep going; no matter how much she hurt, all through her being. She knew her only chance to have a life was to outlive them; no matter what. She could pick up the pieces later—God said she had all of eternity to do it. Just like her parents taught her. They were the ones who taught her to never give up; no matter how much she hurt. The fools. They shot themselves in the foot.

She remembered her body hurt from being so cold all the time after the accident. She was even cold in the middle of July and August. Would she ever get the chill of death out of her body?

And then there were the days and nights she spent lost out on the snow-covered streets. Tracey believed at times that she would freeze to death before she finally found her way home. What kind of animals put their blind child through such abuse? And what was wrong with all the school administrators and other professionals who were involved in Tracey's life over the years? Why did they allow her to be denied basic treatment and rehab therapy? Tracey held them all responsible. Tracey had some definite opinions about things. Tracey's shoulders slumped from exhaustion as she entered through the doorway into the school a few minutes later.

CHAPTER 2

As Tracey stepped through the door, she stomped her feet on the mat in a vain effort to get the snow off her shoes. Her weak left foot slid out from under her as she stepped from the rubber-backed mat onto the slick floor. She quickly stuck her right foot out to catch herself. She winced as she jarred her spine in the process.

She continued further into the school, turning left to head to her locker.

"Hey, Tracey!" She heard someone call from behind her. They must be talking to her; she was the only "Tracey" in her small high school.

As Tracey nervously turned around, Brenda Smith, a girl she had known most of her life breathlessly rushed up to her. Tracey could see Brenda's face was flushed and her glasses were fogged over from the cold outside. Tracey wore glasses before she lost her sight completely. She didn't miss the hassle of having those things stuck to her face constantly.

"I wanted to let you know senior pictures are coming up. You should plan to look extra nice on Wednesday to get yours taken when the rest of us get ours done. If you miss it for some reason, there will only be one chance for retakes. And, homecoming is coming up. As a senior, you're in the running for Homecoming Queen. You might win it!" Brenda added with a wink as she affectionately squeezed Tracey's arm.

Tracey appreciated her friend's kind words. At least she tried to include Tracey. Tracey was sure her parents wouldn't allow her to go to the dance.

Tracey stood there staring at this girl who had been a good friend of hers before the accident. They drifted apart after everything happened. Tracey was more of a hitchhiker in her class than an active participant. Her fellows somehow always forgot to include Tracey in activities.

Even though it hurt Tracey enormously, she understood. The way her parents and the rest of the adults around them responded to the situation just made it extremely difficult for any of the other students to fully comprehend her situation—or she theirs. This left Tracey alienated from everyone and everything.

She was grateful to Brenda for feeling comfortable enough to reach out to her—even on such a sterile topic. They once shared their most secret thoughts and intimate dreams with each other as little girls and now, here they were, virtual strangers. Would God ever be able to make up for all Tracey and her friends and family had lost over the years? She was banking on it. How long would it take? As far as Tracey was concerned, He owed her big time for all she had sacrificed. And all she would sacrifice in the future as well. This was her lot in life now. And God owed her.

Right after the accident, when her mother laid the blame at the doctor's feet, Tracey could only blame God. She thought they had a deal? She would do her best to listen to His words, no matter how nuts they sounded; and He would bless her with a good life. Tracey lived by this belief. What do you do when that's not what happens? Tracey had to regroup. Sometimes life just isn't fair.

Now, here she was nearing the end of her time in high school. What did her future hold? She knew the Spanish teacher who doubled as the school counselor had been meeting with the other seniors regarding their future plans. Why didn't he schedule a similar meeting with Tracey? Tracey knew why. Because he had no answers for her. He didn't want to be put on the spot by her.

Tracey became so angry over the years. Every time she tried to discuss her future with her mother, she was reminded she shouldn't worry; her parents would take care of her. Tracey wasn't concerned about that. She was worried about how she would escape from them. She didn't want to be forced to give up her free will to her parents just because she was blind. And brain injured. It just wasn't fair. Her mother liked to remind her life wasn't always fair. Well, they would just see about that. Tracey believed in miracles. She had to. She was a walking miracle herself. How much would she have to suffer before she finally received her next miracle? Only time would tell.

CHAPTER 3

When Tracey reached the wall of lockers, she slid her hand across the front of the metal doors counting eight in from the end to locate hers.

Her locker was located along the wall between the high school math and science room and the English room on the other side.

Tracey was friends with both teachers.

She adored Mrs. Julie. Unfortunately, she didn't have her for a single class. Her only interactions with this fascinating woman were in passing.

Mrs. Julie somehow always managed to make a strong impression on Tracey. The young, open-minded teacher who had come to their school fairly recently, within the last couple of years, had come from somewhere far away. She brought her big-city, open-minded perspective with her when she joined this small, farming community.

Every time Tracey was around Mrs. Julie, she was in awe. There always seemed to be something new and exciting this fresh young teacher was up to with her students. Tracey had heard members of the community and the school authorities grumbling about how liberal she was with some of her teaching techniques. Julie enjoyed coloring outside the lines. Tracey got a big kick out of it.

Tracey also knew Mrs. Matt disapproved of Mrs. Julie's techniques. Mrs. Matt was always scolding Tracey if she caught her addressing the other teacher by her first name. Tracey was incensed. Mrs. Julie invited all the students to call her by her given name. Tracey felt like she was being persecuted by Mrs. Matt just because she was jealous that all the other students favored this younger and more hip teacher. It wound up making Tracey very miserable.

Everyone in school not only knew Mrs. Julie but her husband as well. At least Tracey heard the other students speaking fondly of Sean; Tracey was probably the only one who had yet to meet this mysterious man who had brought their beloved Julie to them.

Tracey grabbed a notebook and her history book from her locker before slamming the door. She turned around and headed back down the hall, passing the wide-open entryway to the high school from the street on her right side as she rushed by; struggling to avoid running into or tripping over everyone else as they all rushed to their first period classes. Tracey could hear Mr. Geranium on the phone in his office and Nellie pecking away on her computer as she rushed past the high school office. She knew she had two different sets of stairs she would have to navigate in order to get to her first class.

When Tracey finally reached the resource teacher's room, she had to recoil from the shudder that went through her as she walked past the history room. Tracey had a healthy fear of the history teacher. She had known him most of her life; his youngest daughter was in her class.

Mr. Merlyn had a reputation for not tolerating any bull from the students. Tracey had heard stories of him literally bodily throwing students through his classroom door for only mouthing off. Early on, Tracey was put in his class. She was always late and she knew this drove Mr. Merlyn nuts. What was she supposed to do? She was already having accidents when she rushed; it just wasn't safe for her to move any faster through the crowded halls. She had only just that morning nearly tumbled down the stairs again.

As a result, Tracey was in a constant state of fear that she would upset Mr. Merlyn and he might hurl her through his open door next. The day they transferred Tracey out of Mr. Merlyn's room, she was quite relieved.

"Good morning, Tracey," she heard Pat say as she entered the room. Tracey had spent most of her time in the resource room since she entered high school. In the beginning, she was angry at the way her parents and the school officials just shut her away in the basement. Over time as Tracey matured, she realized she didn't have a prayer of keeping up in the "normal" classes with the other students; she had no way to read or take notes of anything. Over the years she and Mrs. Matt had developed a respectful friendship as Tracey eventually wound up spending her entire school day in the special ed room—just because her small-town school didn't make any effort to get her accessible books and note-taking materials. While all her fellows were getting top-of-the-line tutoring and guidance from the other teachers and staff, Tracey was ignored and relegated to the special ed room. Mrs. Matt invited Tracey to call her by her first name when they were alone.

"Good morning, Pat," Tracey said with a hard swallow as she entered the room. It still felt strange calling this woman by her first name. She had always been this larger-than-life authority figure in Tracey's world—at least since she entered high school.

Tracey pulled out a chair as she slung her backpack from her shoulder onto the hard, enamel surface of the community table in the center of the room.

"Remember, you have your teacher aide time in the first grade today. In a few minutes after we say the Pledge of Allegiance and I take attendance, I'll dismiss you to go on up there. Do you need help finding the correct classroom?"

Oh, that was today? Awesome sauce! Tracey thought to herself. "I think I can find it, thanks. I'll just leave the classroom quietly when it's time . . . if that's okay?"

After the morning rituals were out of the way, Tracey quietly left the room gently closing the door behind her.

As she began the long trek back upstairs to make her way to the other end of this sprawling building, she was excited to see the kids. She had been volunteering in the first-grade classroom since the beginning of the school year. Sure, she was only sitting quietly and listening while they took turns practicing their oral reading skills. When the reader mispronounced a word, Tracey would gently interrupt said reader and give them the correct pronunciation of the word. Tracey knew how valuable this practice was. She was an avid reader herself before she went blind. She was thrilled she was able to spend this quality time with these precious children.

Tracey made it up the basement stairs safely. She began to skip as she got lost in thought. Suddenly the earth just went out from underneath Tracey. As she was hurtling through the air, she remembered too late the set of four stairs that led down to the elementary from the high school. Tracey winced in anticipation of what was coming as she braced for impact . . .

CHAPTER 4

Tracey was limping and rubbing her right hip when she reached Mrs. Turner's room. She gently tapped on the door she found slightly ajar.

"Hey kids, look who's here!" she heard Mrs. Turner say as she fully entered the room.

Tracey smiled at the chorus of "hellos" and "good mornings, Tracey" that she heard from the kids.

"Are you guys ready to go read today?" Tracey asked them.

"Yes!" they exclaimed as little Jimmy literally jumped up and down with excitement.

"Bobby and Cindy, get your beginner readers and follow Tracey," Mrs. Turner instructed the first students on the list.

As Tracey walked back down the hall towards the library with the two little ones following close behind, she was amazed at how weird it felt being back at this end of the school where the very smallest scholars studied. Tracey remembered being small and going up into the high school for art class and computer lab and seeing the big high schoolers. She realized she was investing in the futures of these little ones. Would they remember her fondly when they thought back to these early years of life also? Tracey was doing her best to sow seeds that would yield good fruit.

Tracey enjoyed her time with the kids. She would listen carefully while they read—no matter how slow they went. She would gently prod them. Then she would help them sound out the word if they didn't attempt it on their own. She was nearly always able to figure out what word they were struggling with based on the context of the story. When all else failed, she would simply ask the child to spell the word for her and then she would help the child sound it out properly.

Over time she was able to witness a marked improvement in the skills these children demonstrated in their oral reading skills. Tracey always planned on being a teacher when she grew up; someday. What would she do after she graduated in the spring? Just who would she become? It seemed like all the other seniors already knew where they were going in life and what they would do when they got there. What about Tracey?

Her eighteenth birthday was coming up at the end of the month. It just seemed like it should be a significant event. Would God do something really big in her life for this special occasion? She knew her own mother didn't care. Oh well! As long as it was just a plain old ordinary day and not a bad one, Tracey wouldn't complain.

That night as Tracey lay in bed, she thought about what she was going to do. She just had to figure something out. She felt like she was running out of time. The graduation ceremony was planned for some time in May—wasn't it?

CHAPTER 5

On Wednesday morning Tracey dressed in a white cardigan sweater and black slacks. One of her little sisters helped her make her hair nice for her senior pictures. She was all ready for the occasion.

On the way to school, Tracey fell down in a big muddy puddle. This mess was formed as the snow from the last few days melted, refroze and then partially melted again—turning into this hopeless, slippery mess for a blind girl to walk through. It was no shock when Tracey found herself sitting in the middle of it all as her feet slid out from underneath her that day. What was she going to do now?

She would miss the school bus if she went back home to change. So, Tracey was forced to take her senior pictures in her damp, muddy clothes.

The cameraman politely pretended he didn't notice as Tracey tried to place herself at such an angle that the worst of the stain on her clothes wasn't fully visible to the camera lens. Why did Tracey always find herself being forced to pretend her life was normal when it clearly wasn't?

After the photo shoot with the other seniors, Tracey headed for lunch.

As Tracey approached the lunchroom, she was excited. The lunchroom was always interesting.

There was often some new activity going on while lunch was in session.

In the lunchroom, Tracey always just sat wherever she liked. And she visited with whoever she wound up sitting beside until they got up and moved to another table. This often happened to Tracey. The kids in her high school could be so cruel.

The first year her parents sent her to public school after the accident the school provided an assistant for her; someone who read and wrote for her. Ever since they stuck her back in public school, she hadn't been given the same assistance. She was just thrown out there. And she failed at everything that first year.

The only reason she was passing in Mrs. Matt's room was because everyone passed in her class. Everyone got a "participation trophy." She could still barely read anything. Tracey desperately needed a challenge in life—something to get her mind and soul pumping again, at full throttle.

Tracey moved in quick, short bursts through the lunchroom when it was this full. If you didn't, you got stuck or worse, trampled by someone else. It was every man for himself in there, and Tracey was the only blind one. It was rough . . . believe me! It was just about a month ago when Tracey collided with another student who was also carrying a tray full of food. The collision caused quite a mess.

Awesome! They were serving her favorite meal today; burger-in-a-bun.

As Tracey went through the line with the other students, she put a healthy helping of mashed potatoes and a scoop of corn on her tray right next to her main course. She took a scoop of applesauce to round off her lunch. After grabbing a pint of chocolate milk from the crate on the floor and silverware from the cart on wheels, she turned to go find a place to sit. The lunchroom was full with everyone talking at top decibels. Tracey was keenly aware of the clatter of heavy, metal utensils as they randomly hit the floor around the lunchroom. The other students laughed and chattered away as they ate around Tracey, barely noticing her presence. Tracey jumped when someone dropped their full tray on the floor making a loud racket. "Oops, sorry," she heard one of the freshmen exclaim from across the room.

"Hi Tracey!" she heard Elsie greet her.

"Hi there, Elsie. I'll see you after lunch," she said with a mysterious wink as the other students stood around watching while this blind student had this private communication with Elsie. All the students knew Elsie. Tracey was one of only a few who had been given the privilege of working beside this interesting woman. As a matter of fact, you had to be a student in Mrs. Matt's room to qualify for the opportunity.

Tracey knew the other kids probably didn't understand what she did in the cafeteria with Elsie and the other cook after they were all gone back to their afternoon classes.

After Tracey was done getting her lunch, she turned around, balancing her tray carefully in her hands as she inventoried the lunchroom. Where should she sit?

After Tracey was seated, she reached out her hand, grasping the bright red ketchup bottle that sat on the table next to the shiny metal napkin dispenser.

Picking up her burger-in-a-bun in one hand, she turned it, feeling for the soft underside. When she found it, she stuck the tip of the ketchup bottle deeply into it, squeezing the bottle tightly so a generous dollop of the tangy condiment filled the cavity of her entrée—just the way she liked it. Then she took a big bite out of it, slowly chewing as she relished the taste of the cooked hamburger, the fresh-baked bun and the tangy ketchup as it melded together in her mouth.

After Tracey was done with her lunch she rose to her feet, carefully piling her napkins, empty milk carton and other garbage on her tray. She turned and walked towards the kitchen where she could scrape her tray in the garbage and put it away with the other students' trays.

Tracey saw Elsie on the other side of the open half wall as the cook washed trays with the fancy industrial-sized washer that seemed to spray water everywhere as far as Tracey could tell.

"I'm going to run to my locker and use the restroom. I'll be back to get to work in a few minutes, okay?" she said to the head cook.

CHAPTER 6

When Tracey returned to the now nearly empty cafeteria, she confidently walked to the other end of the long room into the kitchen where Elsie was still busy cleaning up. She grabbed a clean apron from the drawer, putting it on and tying it behind her waist. Then she grabbed an empty cart, steering it over to the counter where she turned the water on hot so it could begin to run while she waited for it to heat up. After she stuck her fingers in the stream and discovered it was good and hot, she grabbed the industrial-sized bottle of liquid dish soap that sat on the countertop and sprayed a generous glop of it in the bottom of the large, metal bowl she used for busing the tables each afternoon. She stuck the bowl under the spray, sticking her finger over the lip of the bowl so she could feel when the water rose to her desired level. Then she reached into the long drawer at her hip and removed a clean washcloth, sticking it under the spray to wet it quickly. She placed the metal bowl on the top shelf of the cart on wheels. Tracey carefully steered the cart out of the kitchen and into the cafeteria where she got started on her daily duties.

Tracey approached the nearest of the rectangular tables to get started. There were two long columns of tables and she had to bus them all as well as the attached seats on both sides. No one liked sitting in ketchup or other sticky substances when they came to lunch on each new day.

She took the metal bowl off the cart and sat it on the far end of the first table. She wrung out the washcloth and carefully wiped down the table—crossing and recrossing over her work to make sure she did a thorough job of cleaning up after the other students. When she was done with the first table, she would move the cart to the next table where she would repeat the process. She would wait until the end to wipe down all the seats. Tracey also wiped down the napkin dispensers, the salt and pepper shakers and the ketchup and mustard bottles as she bused the cafeteria tables.

After she was done with that, she would carefully steer the cart back into the kitchen where she would put away the cleaning supplies she had used. Then Tracey would stand right next to Elsie and chat with her while she rinsed the trays, stacking them in the drying rack as Elsie finished washing each one. Tracey loved working in the school cafeteria. When she was done, she headed back to Mrs. Matt's room all the way on the other end of the building. Tracey got a lot of exercise at school.

CHAPTER 7

When Tracey entered Mrs. Matt's room, she was thrilled to find the teacher was reading orally to the entire class. Mrs. Matt always read interesting books such as classics or true stories so everyone in the multi-aged classes learned and enjoyed the stories. This small-town school ran their special ed room like a one-room schoolhouse and Tracey loved it. She enjoyed getting to spend time with students of so many different ages.

Today Pat was reading To Kill a Mockingbird. Tracey quietly took a seat at the community table where she could listen with the others. Tracey loved classics such as this. Tracey was amazed at the way they all sat spellbound as they listened to the teacher reading out loud. Tracey had always believed in the power of the written word. Would she ever be able to read it again?

The day she woke up and found herself totally blind; she was horrified. Why did God do this to her? How unfair could He be? He was the one who gave her this zest for learning. And this love for reading. How could He just rip it away from her like He did? Maybe He hadn't . . . She still didn't believe anything the doctors had been saying . . . She had already proven most of their predictions wrong. Why was her mother still so convinced there was no hope for Tracey? Tracey had argued with her mother until she was blue in the face over the years. Tracey was shocked at the way her mother was so convinced Tracey would never be able to live on her own terms—like any "normal" person. Tracey had grown weary of trying to help this ignorant woman see reality. No matter what Tracey did every day, her mother literally believed Tracey was a member of the walking dead. That she was bound to expire eventually; if they just waited long enough. Would Tracey ever get ahead of that stupid diagnosis? That "misdiagnosis" those stupid doctors made regarding her life before she even woke up to defend herself. Would Tracey ever be able to prove to her mother that she wasn't that broken, worthless creature the doctors had left her with after it all happened? She didn't want to spend the rest of her life fighting to prove to her own mother that she was really alive. What was she going to do? She had to escape. There was no future living with a mother who believed you were dead. She was almost eighteen years old. When would she manage her getaway? Tracey began looking for opportunities for escape.

CHAPTER 8

Tracey awoke on Friday to find the subfreezing temperatures had returned. Instead of most of the ground being wet and slippery, it became very cold, and dry. There was this very cold, dry wind blowing across the land. It blew most of the snow away. In its wake, it left this bone-chilling cold that lasted for days.

Tracey's fingers and toes hurt when she walked to school in the morning. Not only the ground but the very air was dry and crisp to breathe into her lungs. Tracey could literally feel the hairs in her nostrils freezing together as she inhaled and exhaled through her nose with her mouth closed. Her lips were sticky from the effort to stay warm. She didn't want to allow any of this super frigid air directly into her lungs; it may lead to pneumonia. Something just told Tracey she shouldn't do that to her body.

When Tracey finally reached Mrs. Matt's room that morning, she was thrilled when she realized it was pop machine day. Tracey always enjoyed Fridays because of this super fun activity.

In the hallway at the top of the stairs that led down to the basement where the resource room was located there stood two machines. One of them distributed Coke products, the other canned juices and teas.

Tracey rarely had any money to get anything from the machines. She realized most of the other students in Mrs. Matt's room didn't either.

On Fridays, the crew from the resource room would inventory the machines to see what products needed to be replaced. They kept track of everything on a spreadsheet that Tracey was unable to read. She wasn't allowed to participate in that part of the process.

Tracey took part in counting and rolling the dollar bills and loose change that came out of the machines each week.

It was loads of fun chatting with the other students while she separated the coins by denomination before stacking them into two rows of five stacks of coins; quarters, dimes and nickels. Then Tracey would reach into the box of coin wrappers that Mrs. Matt picked up from the bank when she made each week's deposit. Tracey would feel around until she found the right size of wrapper for whatever denomination of coin she was wrapping at that moment. Tracey would unfold the coin wrapper, sticking her finger into the end to open it up all the way. She left her finger in there to catch the piles of coins as she dropped them into the top of the wrapper before securely folding them at the ends to keep the coins from falling back out. Each coin wrapper was stamped with the school's name on them by one of the other students. The kids also counted the dollar bills, putting them in stacks of twenty for the bank.

Tracey couldn't even see the currency well enough to recognize President George Washington on them. She was supposed to make sure each bill was facing the same direction. After studying a bill closely in her hand, she realized that one of the round symbols located next to the president's face was shaded differently on one side from the other. This is how Tracey made sure each bill was facing the same way. Everything was supposed to be uniform for the bank.

One of the sighted students wrote everything down on the spreadsheet. Tracey couldn't see any of it. At least Mrs. Matt allowed Tracey to participate. Tracey was never allowed to do this kind of stuff at home.

After the students were done with inventorying and restocking the machines, it was time for Mrs. Matt to pay up. It was on Fridays that she settled up with her students. Mrs. Matt had a neat system in which she would award students for their accomplishments with points throughout the week. On Fridays, the points were tallied up. Once all the students knew how many points they had, they could exchange them for fun things like bouncy balls, stickers, Dum Dums suckers, Starbursts, bookmarks, Jolly Ranchers, and stuff like that. You could even earn enough points to be given enough change to then go back upstairs and purchase your very own drink from one of the machines. It was loads of fun interacting with the other students and working towards rewards this way.

CHAPTER 9

It was in Tracey's senior year that Mrs. Matt introduced this new concept called "study skills."

On Friday afternoons Tracey and a girl from one of the younger grades would get together. They would read an article together. Then they would discuss it and answer a few questions about what they read. They did all of this orally. Tracey could barely read or write anything . . . remember?

Over time, Mrs. Matt came to "trust" that the girls were doing what they were supposed to. They always met on Friday afternoons when many of the other students were out playing hooky anyway . . . What was wrong with skipping out on their study skills classes? It wasn't as if they were graded on their performances. This is the conclusion the girls eventually came to.

At first, they just talked about it; then they decided to do it. Within a week or two they were no longer even checking in with each other and pretending to do anything before skating out of the school for the weekend.

Tracey started becoming nervous. So much so that the day she arrived at Mrs. Matt's room and was solemnly instructed to go upstairs to Mr. Geranium's office she was shaking and nauseous the entire way. Did they know?

As Tracey took her seat in the principal's office and waited for him to get off the phone, she nervously picked at her cuticles. What would happen to her?

"Good morning, Tracey," he began distractedly.

"Last week while you were out of town one of the students in Mrs. Matt's room was caught stealing money from the funds from the soda machines that were being counted. It was young Master Duncan. That boy's family has been through so much, now this . . . Anyway, as part of his punishment, we had a whole school assembly in which we made the announcement so everyone would know. You missed it so I'm telling you now."

Wow! Since when did this guy concern himself about whether Tracey was being left out of anything? And poor Duncan! To be made an example of like that. He was a good kid. He would have only done this because his family was going through such hard times. At least she wasn't in trouble.

Tracey felt sick at the thought.

As Tracey took a shaky breath, she realized Duncan may have been the one who stole cash out of her locker recently. It wasn't much; she didn't have anything. It was just a few dollars she had been saving for a rainy day. Oh well, she would say a special prayer for Duncan and his family when she went to bed tonight. God would take care of them.

It was a few days later when Mrs. Matt confronted Tracey herself. Tracey didn't even try to deny it; she was literally incapable of lying. (She didn't have a "poker face.") She just sat there quietly listening and waiting to hear what her punishment was going to be.

"This will go on your permanent record. You are the oldest student involved here. You should have set a better example for the younger students. Everywhere you go in your future, the fact that you cheated will go before you."

Tracey's only thought was . . . What future? Thanks to these people, she probably didn't have much of a future.

Tracey couldn't wait to get out of this stupid school for good. She was tired of playing their games day in and day out. Someone had to be the grownup in this situation.

CHAPTER 10

In the days leading up to her birthday, Tracey began receiving weird little calls from her biological father. This guy had always made himself extremely scarce in her life. What did he want now?

He started dropping hints about her birthday present. He was clearly quite excited about giving it to her.

"Okay, this is the last hint. It's egg-shaped," he had said just that morning.

Egg-shaped? What the hell was he up to?

Tracey realized years earlier that both her parents struggled to find appropriate gifts for her. Before she went blind it was easy. People who knew her just inquired as to which book she would like for a gift, and they would get it for her. Once she went blind, what then? Even many traditional gifts became worthless to her.

Unfortunately, neither of her parents had acquired the ability to think outside the box. She had grown to hate her birthday and other holi-days as a result. Opening up yet another goofy and worthless item from one of her parents (or other misguided people) just got to be a drag. Tracey hated being forced to pretend that she was elated about another piece of worthless junk. How much of this was due to her age and how much to the obvious chasm that had developed between her and her parents?

What was she supposed to do? How could two people be so disconnected from their own daughter?

Tracey was excited, nonetheless. Her dad was so excited. Maybe . . . just maybe her dad had finally figured something out.

Tracey died inside when she finally opened her gift. It was a tall, rigid, metal pedestal with a large, hollow ostrich egg perched upon it. The shell of the egg had been broken open, the broken shell hinged to create a little door so one could see its inside contents; a cutsie little scene that was only visible to sighted people. What was Tracey supposed to do with this?

"You can feel the shape of the egg with your hands," her father proudly proclaimed; as if he were a genius for thinking of this wonderful gift.

She could tell her dad was disappointed in her less than enthusiastic response. All she could do with it was set it on her dresser—for sighted people to enjoy when they entered her room. Tracey got tired of it being in the way. She dragged that thing around with her for years out of a sense of obligation. She finally donated it to charity during one of her moves later in life.

CHAPTER 11

The day Tracey walked in the door from school and was informed by her mother she had received a piece of mail, she was excited. Who sent her a letter?

"It's from the federal government. They are inviting you to sign up for the armed services; as if you would be any good to the government," her mother added with a cruel snicker.

Tracey just bit back her tears of anger. She realized a long time ago her mother was an ignorant, lazy woman who couldn't see past the end of her own nose. How could she possibly know what Tracey was capable of? She had spent the past six years doing everything in her power to convince Tracey she had no hope. She hadn't succeeded though—thank God!

The day Tracey was assaulted in the bustling hallway at school and not a single witness could be found who would come forward and assist Tracey in her attempts to confirm the identity of her assailant, Tracey finally realized she wasn't necessarily safe at school either. What was going on? How many of the other girls were actually suffering worse than she had and no one was helping them either? Was it possible that God was protecting Tracey from a whole lot of shit by alienating her from her peers the way He had? Tracey was thankful to Him for this.

When her mother heard about the incident at school, she told Tracey it was her fault she was assaulted. If she wasn't bent over in front of her locker like that, the perp would not have seen the invitation to assault her from behind.

Tracey was furious. What kind of sense did that make? Why was her mother making lame excuses to defend the monster who assaulted her blind daughter? She couldn't even count on her own mother for support in life.

Tracey knew she couldn't count on the school administrators either. Tracey was all alone in this fight. What was she supposed to do?

CHAPTER 12

When Mr. Merlin took the other seniors to Washington, D.C. for the "Coast Trip "where they would be touring the White House and the rest of the buildings that make up our federal government, Tracey wasn't even invited. In fact, she was disinvited. She was informed that she would get to hang out at the high school and watch movies the week the rest of the seniors were on the trip. Tracey felt so disenfranchised. Why did all her teachers—these people who had known her most of her life—always count her out? These were educated people. What was their excuse? She knew both her parents were high school dropouts who didn't concern themselves with the education of their children. Would Tracey ever find someone willing to stand in the gap for her? She had a lot on her shoulders that no one around her could even comprehend.

CHAPTER 13

As the weather continued to become warmer, Tracey hurtled helplessly towards her high school graduation with no hope of a future. How could she walk down there with her classmates and get her diploma when she couldn't read, write or even use a computer? She may figure out how to apply for college but what was the point? She had just spent the last four years spinning her wheels in high school and look where that had gotten her? College would be even more demanding. College was out of the question for sure now.

Everyone else in her class went ahead with the typical arrangements.

The day of the graduation ceremony, while her mother was getting her ready she told Tracey she was proud of her. Proud of the fact that she had stuck it out in high school—even though she knew it was difficult for her daughter. Tracey hated her mother for this lame attempt at a peace offering; this attempt to make herself feel better for robbing her daughter of a proper education and normal high school experience. As her mother struggled with the tears of pride she was feeling, Tracey's tears were tears of anger. Would Tracey ever be able to forgive her mother?

EPILOGUE

It took less than two years from the day Tracey "graduated" from high school until the night her mother launched their trap.

Tracey didn't see this one coming and she was caught up in it—possibly forever . . . That was the night she was dragged into court by her four parents and their lawyers for an "emergency" court hearing in which Tracey was stripped of her constitutional rights. She was locked down under an unconstitutional guardianship. It took nearly fifteen years and hundreds of thousands of dollars before Tracey was able to escape from their trap. Why did He do this to her again? He better have a good reason . . .

SO, WHAT NOW?

CHAPTER 1

Penni Plumber groggily opened her eyes. She was immediately blinded by the bright sunlight that streamed through her basement bedroom windows. This just felt wrong from the beginning. Penni didn't question the feeling.

She must be late for school.

As Penni leaped out of bed she ran for the bathroom; she had to take a leak something fierce.

After Penni was done in the bathroom she stopped for a moment and listened. Why didn't she hear her little sisters getting ready for school? The sun was already so high in the sky. Surely it was already past time for them all to leave. Why did they allow Penni to oversleep?

Penni tore up the wooden steps that didn't have backs on them.

Penni could remember what it felt like on the few occasions when she accidentally put her foot through those backless steps in the early years. Those steps were dangerous for a blind girl to navigate in her weakened condition. Penni wondered for a long time if this was one reason her parents had selected this old house for their family after their eldest daughter was suddenly blinded in her youth. It added up in her mind. Penni had fallen down these stairs so many times over the years.

This was the old house her parents had purchased before the lawsuit was settled with money they borrowed from her grandparents; the ones who lived just down the road.

Well, they had lived just down the road. It was just about a year ago now when her grandfather had succumbed to lung cancer.

Grandpa had always rolled his own cigarettes—ever since Penni first met him. As one of his grandchildren, she could clearly remember the red, metallic cans of Prince Albert's tobacco that could always be found on the table next to Grandpa's chair in Grandma's kitchen. Grandma complained for years about the holes Grandpa accidentally burned into her table cloth with ashes from his smoking habit. Penni remembered watching in fascination as he would pull a thin rolling paper from the package before smoothing it out. He was so precise and matter-of-fact in his movements as he gently shook a generous portion of tobacco onto the paper before rolling it up; licking along the edge with his tongue to glue it closed.

Grandpa always had the radio playing next to him when Penni went to visit. She remembered listening to Paul Harvey's "The Rest of the Story" and "Tradio" on Grandpa's staticky old radio. Penni loved it!

When Penni first met him, Grandpa had a circle of white hair left on his balding head. Grandpa lost the last of this hair in his fight to defeat lung cancer.

Another fascinating feature of Grandpa was his false teeth. The old guy had a full set in his mouth.

Grandpa liked to show them off to unsuspecting children.

The first time Penni met Grandpa he spat his false teeth out at her.

Taken aback, Penni instinctively took an uneasy step backwards.

Not to fear. Grandpa expertly caught his chompers in midair—like a pro. It was obvious to Penni this guy had done this before. Grandpa had a knack for finding quarters behind the ears of his grandchildren. Her new grandpa drove the tall, noisy blader that smoothed out the streets. In her youth, Penni and the rest of his grandchildren could often see Grandpa high up in his patrol blader as he drove up and down the gravel streets of their town, smoothing out the ruts. Penni loved her awesome grandpa. He was big and strong until the cancer got him later.

Her new grandma was awesome as well. Grandma hummed or sang almost all the time. Grandma had a cuckoo clock that hung on her wall. At the top of each hour, a different bird would pop out of the little door and sing its own particular song. She had an old crank phone hanging on her wall for her grandchildren to admire at a distance. Grandma also had a birdcage in her living room with a couple of parakeets.

She wore glasses that were tinted when Penni was young. She wore her hair in tight curls under a silk scarf every day. Grandma had a small couch in her living room that she referred to as a "Davenport."

Grandma had a cribbage board that the aunts and uncles used to gather around on family holidays.

When Penni was young, her grandma could always be found in her sewing room making a homemade patchwork quilt for another lucky member of the family. Penni really loved her talented, beautiful grandma. Grandma made potatoes with every single meal. She would eat raw onions whole—like they were apples.

You couldn't go to Grandma's house when Grandpa was alive without finding a freshly baked batch of her world-famous homemade dough-nuts. (Penni wondered for years if this was the only reason Grandpa married Grandma.)

Penni, her cousins and her little sisters were the envy of all the kids in town. Her grandpa put a little playhouse out in the yard that he built for her aunts and uncles himself when they were young. It had served as a fun place for his grandchildren and so many other children over the years as well. It had a stove with burners and knobs you could really turn. It had a wooden door that was hinged that you could open to access the oven. There was a fridge, a cupboard with a built-in two-sided sink with a faucet and nobs that turned, a table and a couple of chairs—all in this little playhouse. There was a window with a "real" plexiglass pane in it and a door that swung on hinges. It was wonderful! Penni and her little sisters enjoyed playing house in it when they went to Grandma's house as children.

There were at least four different lanes Penni and her cousins could take on their bikes to coast right into their grandparents' yard to visit over the years. It was wonderful!

Penni knew her grandma rarely went out these days.

Now, it was just her dear elderly grandmother living there—all by herself.

Penni realized her poor grandma was going blind just like her grand-daughter. Would Penni die alone and helpless in this small town right next to her grandmother? Penni hoped not. She deserved a chance to live her life also.

Her poor grandmother was actually far worse off than Penni. She knew the elderly woman was also nearly completely deaf. How could Penni help her grandma? She couldn't even help herself!

CHAPTER 2

Once Penni made it upstairs she confronted her mother who she found sitting in the living room, watching television. "Why didn't someone wake me up? Now I'll be late for school."

"You don't go to school," her mother calmly responded as she continued to stare at the television, stuffing doughnuts into her mouth.

What? Of course, Penni went to school! It was the law. Penni had always known even her mother couldn't prevent her from getting an education.

What was her mother talking about?

As her mother continued to insist that Penni didn't go to school, Penni once again had a strong feeling she had stumbled into the legendary Twilight Zone. Something strange was going on.

Penni finally gave up with a shrug of her shoulders and went back downstairs.

As Penni walked, she thought about this queer turn of events. She was sure her mother wasn't lying; the government would never let her get away with depriving her daughter of an education, even if that daughter was blind. Penni had always counted on that. Penni began to realize what was going on. She went back into her bedroom where she sat on her bed to ponder these things.

CHAPTER 3

Ever since Penni first came home from the hospital she had been experiencing this dreadful case of insomnia. It was definitely connected to the brain injury. It was a terrible situation!

Penni experienced the identical thing every single night for years. When she first went to bed, she usually fell right to sleep as she was always exhausted long before "bedtime." Then, after her family had gone to bed, Penni would wake back up. And she would be wide awake for hours. She eventually gave up on getting back to sleep most nights and would just get out of bed and play with Sox and Troubles, the family cats, since they were nocturnal creatures also.

Eventually, Penni always went back to bed; she was an obedient child who didn't want to trouble her poor parents any more than she already had in her young life. Penni would lay there in the darkness listening to reading book machine stories until the rest of her family woke up or she fell back to sleep.

There were some nights when Penni would wake up to find herself standing somewhere in the dark basement; she never knew where she might find herself when she came to "full-consciousness." Penni must have been sleepwalking. This happened several times. Often, by the time Penni finally got her bearings in her own home, she would find herself about to wet her pants before she could find the restroom.

Most of the time Penni just felt like she wasn't fully present in life— like her transmission was in need of a tune-up. Where could she find a master mechanic with the vision and tools to help her in life? It felt like her mind, brain and heart needed to be recalibrated. Penni experienced all these symptoms and more through adolescence and well into adulthood.

Needless to say, although this was a new and peculiar development, it wasn't the worst symptom Penni had experienced during all these years she had been living with her brain injury.

It took a couple of days before Penni felt like she was fully present in the here and now once again. She felt like a zombie in the meantime.

CHAPTER 4

As soon as Penni "graduated" from high school the previous spring, her ignorant mother had been forcing her to engage in all kinds of mindless tasks while continuing to deny her further education in an effort to dumb her down even more than they already had through all these years. Penni was extremely angry. She struggled to find ways to stimulate her brain just to keep her sanity.

The knowledge that her own parents were trying to kill her and get her out of the way just drove Penni onward to her healing . . . and eventually her freedom. If they thought they had succeeded in convincing her that her life was over, they had another think coming. Penni knew she had all the time in the world to make herself whole again; this was her one mission in life. She was the "Measuring Life" after all.

The only way to do this right was to survive and even thrive amid all their bullshit. And then, to get her revenge for all they stole from her in the process.

Her keepers were nothing but a bunch of uneducated, gluttonous, blind buffoons who didn't recognize their daughter's efforts to heal herself.

They just laughed at her and threw stumbling blocks in her path. Penni valiantly climbed over or through them all. Until it was too late for them. She finally got the jump on them all.

Penni felt like the tortoise. The lawyers, doctors and her parents were the proverbial hare. Penni would come out in front, eventually. It was inevitable in her mind.

First, she was forced to outthink those inexperienced, narrow-minded doctors as she vanquished that tumor. Later, Penni outwitted those dim-witted lawyers when she beat them at their own game on their home court. It was a marvelous victory!

How did she do these things? All the experts counted her out years ago. How did she finally beat all those doctors, lawyers and other professionals?

It was simple. Penni believed in herself; even when no one else on earth did. She realized she was the only person with a front-row seat to what was really happening inside her. This gave her an incredible edge on the rest of them—on those despicable lawyers and their cronies. Penni could literally write her own future if she wanted to. How could they stop her? She was younger than the rest of them. All she had to do was outlive them. She was bound to win eventually. How long would it take? Penni desperately needed an ally. Where would she find one?

CHAPTER 5

Penni knew instinctively there was more to her than just a scrambled brain and broken body. If she used some duct tape, a lot of God's grace and a ton of hard work, maybe she could rebuild her temple. She needed somewhere to exist.

These were the thoughts that pained Penni all those years while she argued and debated with the doctors and the rest of those idiots. Why was Penni wasting her time debating with these yahoos? She had already proven them all wrong. Penni decided it was her call to make. She was the one with all the difficult work to do. She would never finish this project if she didn't get started. So, Penni started rebuilding herself from day one. She did this for years while they all shook their heads and walked away. Many of them actually threw huge stumbling blocks into her path in an effort to discourage Penni from her mission . . . her mission to recover in spite of and amid all their blowback. Just why was everyone fighting so damn hard to stop Penni from ever getting better? Wasn't that the entire point? There was no hope. They would just use her for what they could get from her before throwing her away—that's what they thought. But Penni had other ideas.

First, she had to escape from her mother somehow.

Penni went to visit her dad and stepmother for Christmas that year.

While visiting the fam, they were discussing Penni's situation.

"If you were to move here with us, we would help you find the tools and training you need to become independent."

So, Penni moved to the other side of the Mississippi.

She saw right away there were many more opportunities here—for everyone else. Her stepmother only locked her in her bedroom instead of helping Penni find the promised help. Penni wound up running away from her dad's house in distress. Her evil stepmother sent the local authorities after Penni.

Penni couldn't believe the crazy twists her life was taking as she sat on that hotel bed describing to those officers what life was like living under the tyranny of her wicked stepmother. They agreed not to tell that bitch where Penni was hiding. Was she on candid camera? If so; this had been an extremely long episode!

Penni's stupid parents just couldn't bring themselves to promote their daughter to adulthood in their minds. Other people usually saw Penni as a whole person when they first met her. Penni spent all her time trying to measure up to the expectations of her own parents. How was Penni going to help her own mother see her for the living, breathing creature she was?

Penni couldn't keep fighting this invisible phantom that had attacked their family in the ambulance that spring day. It just wasn't fair to Penni.

CHAPTER 6

The day Penni saw her stepmother's friend Dave, the gun safety instructor again after several years, his first question to her was, "Why aren't you married?"

Taken aback, Penni felt her mouth fall open as she hung her head in shame. That was a good question. Just why had her parents decided she wasn't worthy of the touch of a man? Penni knew she was a complete woman.

Her mother threatened to forcibly have Penni sterilized every time she thought Penni might be thinking about being with a man. Her parents didn't want her reproducing—this had been made clear to Penni.

Her stepmother had taken a similar approach to that of Penni's mother. What was Penni supposed to do?

Why couldn't Dave see this?

Would Penni ever be allowed to live as a complete human?

Both her mothers were fighting valiantly to keep Penni from becoming a woman. Why?

The situation in her dad's home eventually became so unsafe for Penni that her dad made arrangements for her to go up north and spend time with her grandma. When Penni returned, nothing had changed. Her stepmother was still on the warpath with her sites focused on Penni. That's when Penni planned a trip to Big Sky Country to visit her mother's clan.

CHAPTER 7

Penni flew into the small regional airport that serviced the Hi-Line. Her stepmother's best friend went with to keep an eye on her.

Penni and Kate were having a nice trip. Kate met a couple of traveling salesmen at the hotel. Both women soon found themselves enjoying the company of these charming men.

Kate helped Penni find a machine in the casino attached to the hotel that she could use. Penni delighted in walking down to the casino to play a few bucks when she got bored. Penni could see the bright lights. She thrilled to hear the sounds the machines around her were making.

One day, Penni's machine made one of those fabulous sounds!

One night the women went out for drinks with the salesmen.

Penni told them all she was underage and couldn't get into the bar.

"Don't worry. Our roommate is a bouncer there. He'll get us all in for no cover charge."

Penni found herself surrounded by people who were even younger than herself as she danced the night away at the bar.

Penni and Eric, one of the salesmen hit it off, becoming intimate. At the bar, they danced together. Penni planted a lip-lock on Eric when they were out on the dance floor. Penni was having a nice time as she sipped on a wine cooler. She didn't even like the taste of alcohol; she was only trying to fit in.

Penni received her first hickey that night.

Penni was allowed to explore the hotel solo on that trip. Penni had never been allowed to do anything like what she had been doing on this trip before.

Penni and Kate drove to visit her family on the trip. Penni's family also visited her at the hotel.

Penni didn't see the trap coming. She was just vacationing—enjoying a free life for the first time ever when it happened.

Her scheming mom sprang the mother of all traps on her own daughter.

Penni walked right into their ambush. She had narrowly avoided so many of her mother's traps over the years . . . how had she missed this one?

CHAPTER 8

It was evening. Penni was in the hotel room by herself; Kate had stepped out. She wasn't surprised at the sudden appearance of her mother and stepfather at her room door.

"Come in," Penni greeted them.

A moment later, Penni's other parents, the ones from the other side of the river also stepped into the room.

Penni was immediately seized with terror. What was going on? Was it finally over? Had Penni finally lost after all these years?

She had always known someone would eventually come for her. She couldn't believe it was her own parents though. All four of them! What were they going to do to her?

First, they stripped Penni of all her cash, credit cards and identification. They couldn't take a chance that she could prove to anyone what they were about to do to her.

Penni was introduced to a lawyer, just another of her mother's henchmen. He would "protect" Penni in court that night.

Why did Penni need protecting? She had no plans to go into the courthouse that night.

She was dragged in there against her will by her sneaky, thieving parents and their corrupt lawyers.

They stripped Penni of her constitutional rights and property that night. That "guardian ad litem" only protected her parents and their lawyers while they robbed Penni of her property and ultimately . . . her freedom.

Some bogus lawyer friend of Pete's was allegedly in the bar that night (no doubt preying on underage girls himself). He testified that he witnessed Penni drinking that wine cooler. He also saw her plant that lip-lock on Eric.

They "presented" other bogus, trumped-up charges against Penni as well (all just as irrelevant). Penni had no allies to help her that night; the night her parents and their lawyers railroaded her into that bogus guardianship.

Her mother asked the state of Montana to appoint Pete, the lawyer who helped her defraud the federal government in Penni's name, full guardian over her daughter that night.

They had been scheming for years about how to rob Penni of that money. Now, checkmate—they had her!

That court didn't even have jurisdiction over Penni that night. She was a resident of the state of Minnesota. She was only visiting there that night. Penni was literally kidnapped by her four parents, their loathsome g lawyers and the state of Montana. Then she was held prisoner for fifteen years while she was robbed and abused by those lawyers and her parents. The state of Montana sanctioned the entire crime.

EPILOGUE

Becoming as Uncle Remus's Brer Rabbit

I have always been an avid reader. Perhaps this is why I've embraced writing so readily as a form of teaching.

That night, after he was appointed her guardian, Pete put Penni in his car. He drove her all night to Fort Missoula, on the other end of the state.

Penni opened her eyes the next morning to find herself in a strange, new world.

She was taken to a hospital by Pete and her four parents. They had meetings with "clinicians" and other medical professionals that day.

Finally, they went to the apartments where the clients lived while they were in the program.

As Penni, her four parents and Pete were given a tour of the facility, Penni was ecstatic. This was the training program her stupid parents had been denying her for years.

Pete wanted Penni here. There was nothing her parents could do to stop this.

Now, Penni would be given the opportunities the rest of the country took for granted!

As the coming months passed, Penni was given a new cane that was the right length with training on how to use said cane. She was also taught new social skills.

Penni started maturing at a rapid pace. She flourished in the program.

Penni went on to do many great things in life.

She had always known; it just took believing in herself.

The author.

SAVING BETH'S BABY

CHAPTER 1

There it was again. That funny feeling. It made her think of little fishes swimming up to the edge of their tank and ramming their heads against it randomly and repeatedly. Except this tank happened to be the inside of Beth Greene's belly.

The first time it happened she barely noticed it. When it continued, she decided it must be gas. It felt good—like a tender caress along the walls of her abdomen. Just a light tickle.

After several days of this, the light bulb in her head finally blinked on. She rushed to her calendar to see what day it was.

Beth and her new husband Greg had been trying to get pregnant for a while.

No. She hadn't missed her period. It wasn't even due until the day after tomorrow.

The doctor said the first symptom to look for was a missed period. Three or four days of her cycle being late it would be the right time to go do a home pregnancy test and expect the results to be accurate.

There was no point in doing a test for almost a week.

So, Beth told her best friend and her husband she believed she was pregnant for no other reason than that she felt something moving inside of her. They both humored her.

Beth had been regular for a long time. Normally, she would be experiencing all kinds of nasty symptoms by now. Fun stuff like cramping, bloating, low back pain and fatigue. She felt fine though.

In fact, now that she thought about it, she felt better than she had in a while.

Getting married and then moving into the new house was quite a drain on her physical vitality.

She could only imagine what she would experience once she managed to conceive.

The day finally came when Beth could take the test. Beth and Greg were scheduled to have dinner with her parents that night anyway. It just made sense to tell them now so she could do the test with her mother.

That night Beth and her mother sat together in her parents' private bathroom talking as they waited for the results of the urine test to become clear on the developing wand that lay flat on the counter.

"Do you believe you can be a good mother?"

"Oh, yes!" Beth said with passion and certainty.

As they embraced, Beth prayed her mother finally believed in her too.

When the three-minute timer beeped the time of reckoning had come.

"Well, you're pregnant."

CHAPTER 2

Beth was so excited. Motherhood was another life experience she always wondered if she would be allowed to have.

Beth did the responsible thing and scheduled an appointment with an OBGYN to begin her prenatal care.

At the first appointment, the doctor performed a test to confirm the results of Beth's home pregnancy test. When the results came back, he scheduled Beth to come back in a month for a follow-up appointment.

He calculated an approximate due date for her new arrival, so Beth knew she had about nine months to prepare.

He gave her some free samples of chewable prenatal vitamins and a ten-month script to get more from her pharmacy.

After giving her a complimentary copy of What to Expect When You're Expecting he warmly congratulated her before sending her on her way.

Beth and Greg read the book together as the months went by. They had so much fun talking about each stage of their child's development together.

CHAPTER 3

Beth was starting to show one day when she had a strange encounter with one of their neighbors in her front yard.

Pete was just an alcoholic, a washed-up failed attorney who doubled as the neighborhood bully.

She was standing there minding her own business when he took it upon himself to sidle up close to her while in a drunken stupor. "Don't you think you should go take some parenting classes or something?

I mean, since you've gone and done this anyway?" he said, motioning distastefully at her body.

Beth wanted to punch the bastard in the face for his ignorant insinuations. Beth went out of her way to avoid Pete after that.

Beth had been blind since she was twelve years old. Prior to that, she was her mother's right arm, helping raise her three little sisters while her parents worked long hours. Beth had also provided quality babysitting services to her community for years.

Just who was this arrogant dufus with the balls to challenge her abilities as a mother?

Beth caught Pete rummaging through their mail one day. He scowled at her when she used her iPhone to snap a photo of him reaching into their mailbox with his grubby mitts.

It was a short time later when Greg caught Pete peeking in their bedroom window with a video camera while Beth was changing for bed.

"We have to do something!" Greg exclaimed before he left for work that night.

Beth was trying to calm her husband down.

The next morning Pete knocked on the door of their trailer. "This is my girlfriend, Marjory. We met at the club last night," he proudly said to Beth when she opened the door.

"Okay . . ." Beth said at a loss.

"Oh! I forgot the best part! She's a social worker with the state. She's going to help keep an eye out for you while you're in this . . . condition," he said as his eyes grew wider at how large her body was becoming.

Beth spent at least an hour that night trying to assure Greg Pete and his girlfriend wouldn't become a problem.

It wasn't long before Marjory was back, insisting one of her friends be allowed to "support" Beth around the house. Marjory, as it turned out, had a slew of weird friends from church herself; each available to work in Beth's new home around her family. It wasn't long before Greg and Beth's personal belongings started disappearing as Marjory's friends literally cleaned them out while Greg was at work.

It all started adding up when Beth found out her mother had been hanging out at the Bamboo Lounge with Pete and Marjory. They were known to go back to Marjory's bungalow on the coast for orgies and other illicit activities on the weekends. What were Pete and her mother thinking?

CHAPTER 4

At the end of the first trimester, Beth suddenly became extremely horny.

Beth couldn't get enough of Greg.

"Honey?" she crooned in Greg's ear as he dozed. Beth gently shook Greg. "Wake up!"

"Not again! I have to get some sleep."

"Just lay there and hold still. This won't take long." And so it went. And Beth's baby kept growing larger and stronger inside her body.

Beth faithfully took her prenatal vitamins, calcium supplements and ate healthy. She also drank plenty of water, avoiding coffee and soft drinks while getting plenty of rest.

On the day of her first ultrasound, Beth and Greg were sitting in the examining room with the doctor.

Beth gasped when the cold jelly touched her skin. As the doctor spread it around on her abdomen with the probe, a grainy image appeared on the monitor.

Beth felt like she was able to see the image of her baby herself as she listened to the doctor explain to Greg what they were looking at on the screen.

". . . and over here we have . . . his little winky. I'm 98% sure you are going to have a son. Congratulations, Mr. and Mrs. Greene."

Beth was shocked. God was giving her a son.

Beth was the oldest of four girls. All her mother's other grandchildren were girls. Beth knew her mother had asked God for boys but always got only girls.

Beth felt very loved by God when she thought about what He was entrusting her with.

Looking through the book of baby names was loads of fun. Now that Greg and Beth knew they were having a son, they began researching good and strong male names.

Beth decided to name her son after the first king of Israel because of his faithfulness to the Lord and his bravery in life. She prayed her son would embody these characteristics in life as well.

Greg and Beth also got more serious about setting up the nursery for their new arrival.

One day Beth was out shopping with her best friend. They were stopped at a red light downtown when Beth heard a loud squeal of tires—just before the impact. They were rear-ended.

Beth's best friend was also pregnant. Both their babies flipped over in their wombs that day and laid on their sciatic nerves. Beth could feel her baby's head between her legs when she walked. Shortly after that, both women wound up on bed rest for the remainder of their pregnancies.

Damn! Beth's pregnancy had been awesome; not a single day of morning sickness and now this!

CHAPTER 5

Beth's due date was Christmas Day. At the recommendation of her doctor, she scheduled a C-section about two weeks before.

Beth and Greg got up early that morning.

Beth didn't eat or drink anything before leaving for the hospital, per her doctor's instructions. "Just in case you have a reaction to the medicine, we don't want you having food in your stomach you may choke on if you vomit while recovering from the procedure."

Beth wasn't worried. She had endured a lot of "procedures" in her time—never experiencing any adverse effects from anesthesia.

Beth was laying there on the operating table with a drape over her waist. She was listening as the doctor and his staff worked down around her waist.

They numbed her; it was weird. Beth could feel a gentle but insistent tugging on her flesh down there but no pain while they were performing the C-section.

"Here he comes!" she heard the doctor say. "Wow! What a big boy!" she heard one of the nurses exclaim a moment later.

Beth suddenly heard a loud cry; the first sound her son uttered in this world. It was quickly followed by silence.

"Beth, start praying!" she heard Greg's voice command from the shadowy gloom that surrounded her.

Beth had no idea what was going on around her. She just opened her mouth, crying out to God right there in the OR. She asked Him to spare her son and not to take him from her.

As Beth continued to pray, she heard a loud scuffling in the room followed by silence. All she heard was the sounds of the machines in the room.

"Hello?" Beth said in confusion.

"Just a minute," she heard a nurse's aide say from nearby.

"Beth, your son turned blue after the doctor cut the umbilical cord. The OR team jumped into action, performing CPR on him. They just rushed out of the room with him. I'll go find out what's happening. I'll be right back."

Beth was so frustrated. Here she was laying on this cold, hard table half naked with her privateness all uncovered. She quietly wept as the fear, humiliation and confusion overwhelmed her. Where was her baby and what was happening to him?

CHAPTER 6

When the nurse returned, she found out her son was in the NICU.

"When can I see him?" was all Beth wanted to know.

"After we get you cleaned up, we'll put you in a wheelchair and take you in to see him."

Beth could feel her bottom lip begin to quiver again. She was about to start bawling all over again. Man, she had to get a grip!

"Can I go to the bathroom?" Beth asked sometime later when she woke up again.

"Sure. Just a minute and I'll get somebody else, and we'll come to help you."

As Beth sat up with help sliding her legs off the bed, there was a nurse on each side of her, helping to steady her as she struggled to get to her feet.

"We need you to pee in this cup so we can check your urine," one of the nurses said as she shoved a plastic-wrapped cup at Beth. "Just twist the lid to remove the cover, pee in the cup up to the fill line, replace the lid and open the door on the wall behind the toilet, placing it in there. Someone will remove it on the other side."

Where was her mother? Did her family even know what had happened?

Beth felt so alone, and shattered. It felt as if her guts were just hanging out of her stomach—like someone had sliced her stomach muscles horizontally and vertically before just leaving them hanging in tatters.

Beth felt a burning sensation as she urinated in the bathroom a few minutes later. Was there blood in her urine? She wished she could see well enough to know.

Her head was pounding. She was exhausted, and her heart was broken. She prayed silently as she washed her hands after blowing her nose.

"Are you ready to go see your baby?" Beth heard a cheery voice say.

"Oh yes!" Beth cried.

CHAPTER 7

Beth did her best to stay covered as she was pushed in a wheelchair by a volunteer through the hospital. She sipped on a bottle of water to help rehydrate herself.

"Here we are at the NICU. Now, here's the procedure you and your husband have to go through each and every time you go in to see your son. Everyone who goes in with you has to follow these same procedures to protect the babies in the NICU who are immunocompromised."

After they both washed their hands with soap and water, they put cloth masks over their mouths and noses before entering behind a heavy, coded door that locked automatically behind them.

"You have to keep that wrist band on your wrist. It has a blue tooth code implanted in it that will recognize you and let you back in to see your son. If you don't have it, it will be much harder getting back in here later."

When Beth got close to her baby, she knelt down to get a closer look at him. He wasn't making any noise. All she could hear was the beeping and whirring of the machines and computers that surrounded them.

"Why isn't he making any noise?" Beth asked, puzzled.

"He has a respirator tube shoved down his throat to help him breathe. Your son can't make any noises with his vocal cords at this point."

Beth was horrified. Her poor baby boy! She gently felt around on his tiny form, examining the wires and tubes taped all over his body. She felt his small fingers curl around her long one as she hesitantly touched him.

She bent at the waist, brought her finger to her lips, and kissed his tiny digits she found curled there.. She whispered in his ear, "Mommy loves you and so does Jesus. I'm praying for you, my brave and strong little boy. I'll be back later." Beth gently pressed her lips against his tiny forehead as she silently prayed in her heart.

After that Beth made trips back and forth from her room to the NICU several times a day to see her baby.

The day they kicked Beth out of the hospital because her insurance was done paying for her care following her surgery, she was forced to leave her newborn son behind . . . all alone.

Beth was choking with emotion as she fled the hospital that day.

Beth's life became a nightmarish hell after that. All the trips back and forth to the hospital to take care of her baby on top of what Beth was already dealing with at home left her in an exhausted daze.

One day Beth showed up at the hospital to find her mother-in-law quarreling with the staff at the NICU.

"You can't just come barging in here, ma'am. You have to have a special clearance," Beth heard the frustrated nurse trying to explain to Pam as she insisted she was going in there to see her grandson.

"Pam, remember I called you the other day and told you Greg or I would be happy to take you in to see him; you just need to let us know," Beth reminded her crotchety mother-in-law.

"He'll be home before Christmas, mark my words! The Lord will heal him!" Beth heard Pam insisting to the hospital staff as she stomped away, followed by one of her weird little friends from church.

Beth's son was seven days old when she received a call from the nurse's station in the NICU. "If you want to hold your son for the first time, you and your husband better get over here. We just took the respirator tube out of your son's throat. He's breathing on his own now!"

Beth was shocked. She had been going to visit her son constantly, always praying for him and asking God to let her hold her son just once, please?

Each day was filled with anxiety and frustration as it seemed like she was getting conflicting reports from the staff at the NICU when she went to visit her son. On one visit the attending nurse's aide would assure her that her son was doing great—definitely going to make it. Then, someone on the next shift when Beth stumbled back in later for another visit would say out of their pessimistic outlook that no, things were not looking better for her son. Quite the contrary, as a matter of fact.

How was a blind mother supposed to find hope to cling to under circumstances like those?

Now, she would be able to hold her son at long last and know for herself what his status was!

When they handed her son to her, Beth gently lifted him to her chest, snuggling him up against her breast. She could feel his heart beating and the rise and fall of his little body as he lay against her chest. Her little boy was real, and alive. Thank you, Father, Beth whispered in her heart.

The nurses pushed a rocking chair close to her baby's bassinet so Beth could rock him to sleep each night. Then she would kiss him on the forehead before laying him safely in his crib at the hospital where the nurses and the other angels would watch over him while she went home for the night.

Beth was always back first thing in the morning to get her baby up and change his diaper. The hospital staff grew accustomed to seeing her wander in through the revolving door at the main entrance of the hospital—swinging her long, white cane at all hours of the day and night.

Greg and Beth brought their new son home from the hospital four days after Christmas that year.

All in His perfect timing, Beth thought to herself.

She knew her own mother watched her fight for her life while she was comatose for two and a half weeks when she was a child. Had her mother experienced the same thoughts and emotions Beth had been experiencing these last few weeks?

Beth actually doubted it. She knew her mother struggled with being a woman of faith.

How and why did her mother choose to do this all by herself, without God's wisdom and strength?

CHAPTER 8

The first night home from the hospital was a circus. Beth's baby ran the show—like a pro! He kept his poor parents hopping that night.

Greg and Beth met over coffee the next morning to compare notes and strategize about what happened the night before. They couldn't let a newborn get the better of them.

"Good morning, honey," Beth greeted her husband.

"What a night," Greg said in response.

"I don't know about your idea of sleeping in shifts. It seems to me we should teach our baby to sleep when we do; like normal people sleep. We can't go on like this."

"You know what the trouble is? It's those nurses at the NICU. They are awake in there all night playing with these babies. Then we poor parents bring our newborns home and they want us to stay up all night playing with them also, just like the nurses. We don't have a full staff though. There's just the two of us."

Beth realized Greg may be right. She didn't like listening to his constant whining though. This didn't change their current circumstances. In her mind, it made perfect sense their newborn son might need a couple of nights adjusting to being at home. She was getting tired of her husband's lousy attitude about everything. He had no patience for anything when it came to the baby.

Beth realized she was suffering from ever-growing sleep deprivation as the weeks went by. This is why she found herself mindlessly fumbling around with her son's carrier one day. When she found a small, plastic piece of something or other just lying there, she lifted it to her nose, sniffing it.

What was this? It must have fallen off his carrier. Oh well, she would ask Greg about it when he got up.

The tiny fragment fascinated her until Greg got up a short time later.

"Honey, what is this?" Beth said as she held it out for his inspection.

"Oh, that's the baby's belly button. It must have finally fallen off."

Beth squealed in horror. She had been mindlessly playing with this little thing all morning and now she finds out it was part of her baby!

One day shortly after the baby was home from the hospital Greg had a conversation with Beth. "Do you feel those dents in your newborn's head?" he demanded.

"Yes," Beth replied.

"If you look closely, you can still see black and blue marks on his head—almost three weeks later and they line right up with the dents. I think that doctor hurt our boy when he performed that C-section. I think he grabbed our baby's head with the forceps, squeezing it tightly and causing him to inhale amnionic fluid. That's how he got fluid not only in his lungs but in the lining of his lungs also, causing the wet lung."

When Beth examined her child for herself, she had to admit it looked like Greg may be right. "We should sue that bastard, just like your mom did when you were a kid," Greg ranted.

Beth was overwhelmed with horror at her husband's suggestion. She couldn't let history repeat itself all over again; not with her son.

And not with Pete living so close. She just knew he was looking for another way to get his greedy claws into her so he could go on soaking her for the rest of her life; just as he had done for the decade and a half he was her court-appointed full guardian. What would happen if Pete somehow found out about her son?

Besides, Beth was well aware the federal government instituted a tight cap on how large medical malpractice lawsuits could settle for after her mother's landmark suit when Beth was a kid.

Thanks to his grandmother, there would be no justice for her son or hundreds of other Americans who were hurt by the actions of inept doctors.

If Greg thought he was going to use their child to do the same thing her mother did to her, he had another think coming.

Worse yet, if Pete caught wind her son was now a candidate for his own medical malpractice lawsuit, he might never leave them alone.

If Greg only understood why Pete was so chummy with her mother in the first place . . . or what was at stake here. He never listened when she tried to tell him about the relationship between Pete and her mother. They were thick as thieves, those two, literally.

CHAPTER 9

When Beth rubbed her son's back while singing sweetly to him and rhythmically patting his diapered bottom, he finally began to nestle his body close to her heart and drifted off to sleep. Over time Beth found many different ways to help soothe her son.

Beth and Greg quickly settled into a routine at home. Beth would get up with the baby at night while letting Greg get a good night's sleep. He was the one who went to work every day, after all.

Then Beth would spend the day taking care of and singing to and playing with her baby while doing housework when Greg was gone. In the evenings and on the weekends Greg would make himself available to help with the baby any time Beth wanted or needed a break, which wasn't very often. Beth loved being a mother.

The baby was a few weeks old when Beth and her husband received an unwanted visit from their rude neighbor Pete.

"Hello there. How's the little one doing?" Pete asked as he walked right in their front door one day; like he owned the place.

"Pete, what's going on here?" Greg demanded, coming up behind him.

"Hey! Stay away from me!" Pete snarled at Greg, whirling around.

"This is our home. You can't just come barging in here like you own the place."

"Think again, cowboy," Pete said, slapping a thick legal document against Greg's chest before turning and stomping out the door. "You've just been served. See you in court."

CHAPTER 10

"What is this?" Greg asked puzzled as he stood there in shock, clutching his chest.

Beth took the ridiculously thick document from him, walking to her CCTV and flipping it on. As she scanned through the legalese on the first page, she realized Pete and her mother had just declared war on her and her new family. Her mother and Pete were taking her to court again. This time for a "review of spending" hearing before the judge. The last time it was a bogus capacity hearing on the other end of the state. She knew she wouldn't be granted adequate representation once again.

Pete always made sure the system was stacked against her. Beth could see right through this attempt of theirs to take ultimate control of the money they were both so hot and bothered to get their grubby mitts on. Beth realized her mother probably wanted to steal custody of her newborn son from her as well. He was her only true heir, after all.

How was she going to protect him from her mother's sinister greed? Beth was aware of how much she had already lost because of that damn pot of money Pete and her mother wanted. Beth was only a child—watching all those stupid grownups trying to be sneaky while defrauding the federal government in her name.

Beth realized the time had come to level with her husband. He needed to be ready if they were going to battle.

"You better sit down."

"What is it?" Greg asked, puzzled by his wife's terror-stricken expression.

"It's a long story. It started in 1989 when I was just twelve years old . . ." she began her tale.

"I woke up in this new, scary world in which I was helpless, and no one recognized me. My own mother believed I was dead."

Beth told him about the terror and helplessness she felt when it first happened. "All I knew was I could trust God—only God. No one else was making any sense when they talked."

Beth went on to describe to her new husband what she could only refer to as "the dark years" when her family was broken and hurting, and she was lost in this new hell all by herself.

"During that time, my mother had one of those free consultations with an attorney."

Then Beth described to her new husband how things changed after the lawyers got involved.

She talked about how she assumed things would get better after the lawsuit was settled, but she was wrong.

"It was like everyone's only focus was on figuring out how much money they could get because I had gone blind, etc., etc. All this while I was struggling to go to public school without a cane, with no braille training or support of any other kind."

Beth could feel the anger and passion welling up inside her as she told her husband about all the years of lost time and aptitude—the years she felt had been stolen from her by the ignorance of her parents and the greed of those effing lawyers.

"And then, after denying me access to a proper education and rehab therapy for my dual injuries, when I was 20, they dragged me into court late one night."

She went on to tell him the whole sorted affair. She shared with him this incredible burden she had been carrying all these years.

"I can't rest until I get my full revenge on them for what they have stolen from me," she declared with tears shining in her eyes as she smiled sadly at him.

"Pete was the lawyer who helped my mother defraud the federal government in my name when I was a child. Then, my mother had him appointed my full guardian that night in court. This gave them both unfettered access to my life and account. They robbed and abused me for years. I finally managed to escape from them a few years ago. Pete's been stalking me and my account ever since."

Greg was silent for a moment. "I'm not surprised. Your mother told me about your money the first time I met her when we went up north to camp with your folks at Tiber Dam that first summer . . ." he continued.

Beth was pissed. Her stupid, greedy mother! She put her disabled daughter in jeopardy by blabbing information like this to a total stranger.

Beth was sick of the double standard when it came to Pete and her mother.

CHAPTER 11

The next day Beth started trying to figure out what to do. She began thinking about the problem.

To tell the truth, Beth had already been working on how to solve this little problem for quite some time now. It had become a mammoth disturbance in her life—this guardianship. Maybe it was time to take it out for good.

Besides, Pete was forcing her to get more serious with his full-court press. If Pete wanted a fight, she'd bring it to him, in spades.

As far as Beth was concerned, Pete was nothing but an ignorant, narrow-minded, weak man—just like so many of the other men she had dealt with in the flyover zone. Many of them had no imagination. She decided the fact he believed he was smarter than her would be his downfall.

Beth knew she had already outwitted this idiot and the rest of them years ago.

Just by believing in herself, she beat him—the big dumb loser.

This time it would cost her so much more . . .

The first thing Beth did was hit her knees. She knew where to turn for answers when she really needed the right ones.

After a word of prayer, it suddenly occurred to Beth her pastor was a something or other with the state; wasn't he? Maybe she should give him a call.

Her pastor had expressed his own frustration to her regarding this situation she found herself trapped in. He became aware of it when he counseled her and Greg for their premarital counseling.

"I'll definitely go to court and testify for you and Greg; you can count on me."

This conversation eventually led her to Tad, the rookie lawyer she hired to help her go after Pete and his cronies. There was quite a conspiracy built up against her by then.

CHAPTER 12

The day Tad informed Beth that he expected her to go to the courthouse and talk to the clerk about getting access to the sealed files, Beth was terrified.

How could she go near the courthouse? Bad things happened to good people in courthouses; Beth knew this from personal experience.

She had to do it though. It was expected of her.

Beth always rose to the occasion; no matter what the challenge. Failure just wasn't an option.

Hmmm . . . maybe that's why He called on her in the first place? Because He had designed her to get shit done!

The day Beth walked into the large, echoing courthouse, she was trembling and nauseous. She listened for the roaring of lions as she stepped into this lion's den. Could she bring these ferocious creatures to heal like Daniel did by speaking with the authority of the living God?

She dropped her cane as she fumbled to open the heavy doors on her way in.

As she listened to her steps echo through the large, spacious atrium she strained to hear voices. Where was she supposed to go? She had never been in the courthouse by herself. She was always accompanied by at least one damn lawyer.

Beth really despised lawyers. Most of them would slit your throat when you weren't looking if they got the chance. She had grown weary of having to watch her backside around them. She was just one blind woman, fighting all those corrupt lawyers . . . She was still so angry they were forced into her life when she was so young . . . Would she ever eliminate their influence and presence from her life?

"Hello?" she said when she finally heard voices.

"Oh . . . Hello there. Can I help you?"

"Uh, yes. I have an order here from this judge, granting me access to these sealed records in my case file . . ." Beth started, struggling to hold back her anxiety about courthouses as she tried to communicate to this nice lady what she needed.

"Yes. I can help you. Can I please see the judge's order?"

Beth nervously handed her the envelope Tad gave her the day before when he dumped this horrible errand in her lap.

The woman took a closer look at Beth, at her watering eyes and trembling body. She was concerned at the obvious trauma this poor blind woman was experiencing.

"Well, it's no problem at all. I'm happy to help you. Please have a seat."

Beth nervously sat down while the woman left the room to go find the records.

"This is an extremely old case . . . I may not be able to find anything in here. I may have to go into the archives so this may take a while."

When the woman returned later, she was excited.

"I found it! I found the records from the original case as well. I didn't think I would; the original action was so long ago . . . As it turns out, these case files can never be erased. Your mother set a new record with her landmark settlement against the feds. The story is now part of the historical record of the state of Montana."

Beth was shocked. What was going on in her life? Why did everything have to be so big and monumental all the time?

Beth felt pride at her mother's accomplishment though—at the way she fought so hard for her daughter she left a permanent mark on history. Did her mother know? An even better question: would Beth be able to leave her own indelible mark on God's cosmic calendar?

Beth could see what was coming in her life. Her outlook had become so broad and her perspective so wide; she believed she saw the next several years of her life that day.

It was a bright outlook if she continued to believe in herself. What was coming next in this incredible, blew journey?

Beth was pretty sure she knew. She was so excited to live every minute of it.

CHAPTER 13

When Beth got home from the courthouse, she called Tad. "I got it!" she told him triumphantly. She knew this was only the first of many difficult steps she would have to take on this journey to get her rights back from Pete.

"Fabulous! Can you bring it to my office in the morning? Then we will go over the contents together."

The next morning Beth was sitting in Tad's office while he read the contents of the file aloud to her.

Beth was fuming. Her ignorant, stupid parents! This entire nightmare was orchestrated by their obsessive need to protect that money they sued for when Beth was just a child. They stole fifteen years of her life for this bullshit!

The four letters were written to that judge in Montana. They were full of ridiculous assumptions and lies from her parents; the four people who had set her up to take this fall in the first place.

After being locked in her room for years and denied treatment for her injuries and then a decent education on top of it all, what else did they expect from her?

How the hell had all four of them turned on her at the same time though? Not one of them believed in her?

It was those damn lawyers. And their promises of big money for her parents. Would she never escape this nightmare?

Beth was hurt not even her stepparents understood her. They were broader minded than her biological parents; Beth had known this all her life.

Her mother and father were a couple of dingbats.

But Beth couldn't even count on her steps.

Well, fuck them . . . all four of them! She would have to take care of Pete on her own. She remembered how it felt that night in court. That night when she turned to look for her parents as total strangers put their hands on her and led her away—like a common criminal.

Beth was shocked when her choices were just robbed from her like that by her stupid, blind parents. They were playing right into Pete's greedy mitts.

What was her crime? She had done nothing wrong, except survive that brain tumor. The one that was supposed to take her out when she was just twelve years old. Beth knew that by surviving it and then recovering and moving on with her life, she was proving those lawyers screwed the federal government when she was a kid. They couldn't let this happen. They decided they would frame her for incapacity and take her constitutional rights away.

She just had to stop them. And after that, she would make them sorry they did this to her.

Obviously, the time had come to school them on how they should treat someone like her—those ignorant lawyers.

CHAPTER 14

This was war, on all fronts. Beth realized she couldn't even count on her parents to help her in this fight. They had proven themselves to be cowards and thieves. Beth wasn't afraid though. She looked death in the eye when she was just a kid and lived to tell about it. What was so scary about this clown, Pete anyway?

"So, what's our strategy?" Beth asked Tad.

"You're clearly not incapacitated. I can't believe this was done to you. That court didn't even have jurisdiction over you that night. You were a resident of the state of Minnesota. All your property was there. You were literally kidnapped by the state of Montana and then held prisoner for fifteen years. They seized your property and gave it to that jerk of a lawyer. It's clear how corrupt this was. If this can happen to you, it can happen to anyone who chooses to go on vacation."

Beth was shocked. She was right all these years. They really had done her wrong that night—her parents and their effing lawyers.

What were her choices? She could never get those lost fifteen years back, or the hundreds of thousands of dollars that went into the pockets of those sleazy lawyers and their cronies all those years. She had only one option. She would make them pay.

First, she had to take care of this guardianship her parents locked her in.

Tad continued, "You're clearly not incapacitated. We'll simply challenge the guardianship."

Beth was shocked. Challenge this monstrosity that had taken hold of her life? Hell yeah!

"First, if I'm going to represent you, I need a retainer."

"How much?" Beth asked nervously.

She didn't have much money in her savings. Pete had her living hand to mouth each month.

"Well, judging from your wardrobe, you're not exactly rolling in cash . . . If you can give me $100, we can get started."

Beth smiled at Tad and offered him her hand. "It's a deal!"

"The first thing I want you to do is to sit down and make a list of all the counties you think we should look in for records. This legal mess spans several decades. I'm sure they dragged you all over the state. That's how these sleazy guardianship lawyers usually operate."

"Sure. I can do that."

"And then we will contact each of the courthouses in those counties and get all the files pertaining to you sent to us here."

That night Beth told Greg about her visit to the attorney's office that afternoon. "He said it's clear I'm not incapacitated, and we should just challenge Pete and Mom," she was telling him.

"I've been telling you for years you're not incapacitated. I ought to know; I'm married to you after all. But you needed a lawyer to tell you this? The only reason they did this to you was to get their hands on your money."

Beth was elated the following week when she opened correspondence from Tad. Inside she found a motion to terminate the guardianship. There was a second document included. It was a motion asking the court to force Pete to pay Tad's fees in full. Pete, after all, had been appointed keeper of Beth's money.

Beth smiled to herself. Finally, Beth had someone who was able to stand up to Pete. She started to breathe a little easier. Pete had been a thorn in her side for a long time. Having Tad to run interference for Beth was awesome!

CHAPTER 15

When the boxes of files started arriving at Beth's house, she was a little overwhelmed. There were boxes all over her house. They were stacked on the couch, along the wall in the hallway and all over the floor in the living and dining rooms. (It was a mobility nightmare.)

How was she going to read through all these boxes of files? She could barely see her hand in front of her face. Thank God, He gave her a CCTV.

Well, she would never finish this project if she didn't get started.

With a heavy sigh, Beth reached for the nearest box, sliding it nearby so she could begin examining its contents. She promised herself she would look at each and every document and piece of paper she found in these boxes—no matter how mammoth or insignificant they might appear to be. And no matter how long it took. In these boxes were the answers to many of the questions she had always harbored in her heart. Questions about how it happened and why.

She opened the nearest box. Beth began by dividing the documents into three piles.

The first pile was made up of everything medical. She put all the doctor's reports, medical exams, therapist's reports and anything else pertaining to this part of the nightmare into this pile. (This was what He did to her.)

All the strictly legal shit went into the legal pile. (These were the crimes committed against Beth by those lawyers and the rest of that broken system.) Then there was the third pile. This was the pile she wasn't quite sure about. She would ask Greg to help her get a closer look at those documents later.

Beth decided to read the medical stuff first. This whole thing started in that hospital room when she woke up—after all. What would have happened if she hadn't survived that spring storm? Who would He have given this assignment to?

Beth was fascinated by what she read and everything she learned about what she survived. No wonder her mother and those stupid lawyers were so angry.

Beth was angry too. She was angry this was done to her in the name of protecting that damn money from her. Technically, this money was awarded to her for what she suffered. Why did all these lawyers decide they should be able to take it from her now? She was the one who survived all this bullshit—not them. They only specialized in shoveling more shit into her life, until it buried her alive once again. This was her prize, not theirs.

She was just angry they were making her fight for it all over again. First, she had to survive that tumor and everything that went along with it. Then, those stinking lawyers decided to toss her in that prison they called a guardianship for fifteen years and really give her a project—another big monster in her life she had to defeat and escape from.

Why would they do this to someone who had already had to suffer and overcome so much in life? This is why Beth despised lawyers. They are bullies and thieves who prey on the weakest in our society.

Thank God, He showed her how to change her perspective from one of victimhood to one of victory.

You know; that's how she outsmarted them in the end. And in the beginning. It was in the beginning—on that very first day when she woke up in the hospital, she realized she had just been handed her life's work—like it or not. This was the teacher He wanted her to become.

She believed she had the ability to outthink those educated lawyers from day one as well. So, she did!

It wasn't difficult. She simply believed in herself while everyone else wanted her to just give up and die. How could they possibly compete with her in this realm? They had no way of getting inside her mind and heart to steal her thoughts and dreams. The contents found there had grown exponentially over the years until they were so broad and so vast those slimy lawyers would never make it back inside. They couldn't steal her life from her again.

More importantly, they had forgotten about the law. Their only focus was screwing Beth. Beth put her focus on the law. She understood God's law as well. Beth realized this gave her a massive edge over the rest of them.

Those dumb, lazy lawyers. Maybe it took her years. Maybe it looked like she lost the first time. She finally outwitted them though. Those ignorant, corrupt lawyers.

She knew she wasn't supposed to survive all those years of neglect and abuse that followed the removal of that brain tumor. If she had just given up and died like she was supposed to there never would have been the need for the guardianship trap in the first place. Beth had always wondered whose brainchild that was. Who decided taking her life from her was justified? Was it her mother? Or Pete? She would probably never know. She knew none of these small-town idiots could have thought of it on their own.

They just had to protect that money somehow. You couldn't blame them. It was a religious experience for her parents and their greedy lawyers.

Unfortunately for them, Beth outwitted them all. Now, she had her pen and her stage. She would share her story with the entire world. And get her revenge on them in the process.

CHAPTER 16

She started on all the legal documents next, the ones those busybody lawyers generated all those years. Those years when her parents and their lawyers kept her locked in her bedroom with no access to the outside world. She also read the documents from all the years of the guardianship. Over time Beth got her hands on and read through the files from at least four different courthouses located throughout the state. She also read through the files from the attorneys who fought the original case. Then she read all the bogus files from the guardianship.

It was quite a task reading through all that shit. Lawyers like to create a lot of paperwork. She had to do it though. She was like a starving woman feasting on food—food she had been denied for over two decades.

Her mother and those lawyers never let her in on anything. All those years they ran horrible, painful tests on her, never sharing the results with her.

On the rare occasions when a provider would attempt to bring her in on the conversation, she was usually summarily dismissed out of hand by Marjory, Pete and her parents—her input deemed irrelevant.

The day Beth realized she was the most relevant person in the room was the day she figured out how to defeat all these greedy lawyers, her parents and the rest of these stupid ostriches. She knew there was no way they could fathom the depth of her loathing for them. Or how vast her imagination had become when it came to dreaming of different ways of how she would get her revenge on them. Recovering from that monster-sized brain tumor was no longer her greatest accomplishment. Surviving those greedy lawyers and her ignorant parents was!

They better brace. That's all Beth knew.

Beth got shit done. She didn't run scared in the middle of a project.

CHAPTER 17

As the U.S. emerged into the 1990s, Beth was given another gift from above to help her in her quest to outthink those doctors and lawyers. If people could be born in the wrong body why was it such a stretch of the imagination that Beth was evolving into a new creature herself?

Beth used this logic to cement her faith and fuel the manifestation of her dreams into what He was doing in her everyday life. This is when Beth began to identify with the struggle of the alphabet community. She herself was first misdiagnosed by those stupid doctors and later she was misidentified by those corrupt lawyers. She definitely understood the frustration and anger that was tied in with being mislabeled.

So, you see, Beth literally beat those lawyers and experts using her broken, scrambled brain. She outthought those overeducated retards!

It was however a marathon that spanned almost two and a half decades by the time she was done. Beth was angry. She was angry she was forced to spend so much of her life fighting to justify her existence to a bunch of narrow-minded lawyers. What right did they have? She was a woman created by God. What made them think they were qualified to sit in judgment of this beautiful, mysterious creature?

Beth used the strength she found in these secret thoughts to keep empowering herself to overcome all the naysayers she came across over the years. If they weren't on her team, their perspective was irrelevant in her book. Her book was the only one that mattered.

They couldn't overcome her powerful mind. As time passed and she continued to prove them wrong, they resorted to calling her names. They put labels on her. Terms like "naïve," damaged," nar-cissistic "manipulative" and "impulsive" . . . But Beth knew these were just words, just like the incapacitated label they tried to saddle her with. Beth knew her truth. And that's all that mattered. She would keep up this fight until the end . . . even if the end was the end of her life.

CHAPTER 18

Beth's son was a couple of months old when he caught a spring cold.

Her son struggled with his breathing on a good day. Now, the gasping and gurgling sounds her son was making at times nearly drove Beth over the edge. She wished she could see him better!

Beth was in the kitchen washing bottles one day while her son was engaged in watching the baby channel and swinging in his baby swing. She knew he had dozed off a while ago. Beth could hear the music from the children's program.

Suddenly her son began coughing violently again, to the point of choking. This had been going on for days. Beth was becoming increasingly concerned for her son as those days passed. Now, she went into a panic as she listened to her son struggle for air as he coughed to the point of choking on phlegm.

Beth ran and grabbed her cell phone. She quickly dialed 911.

As Beth listened to the ringing on the other end of the phone, she prayed for her son.

"911! What is your emergency?" came the voice on the other end of the line.

Beth told the operator her son was having trouble breathing and about his medical history.

"I'll dispatch an ambulance right away."

The crew from the nearby firehouse showed up in their ambulance with their sirens blaring a few minutes later.

Beth rushed to the front door to let them in. She pointed towards the living room when the medics rushed in with their stretcher.

A few minutes later Beth was seated in the front seat of the ambulance while it wove its way through traffic on its way to the hospital. Beth cringed when she heard her son cooing to the paramedics in the back. Had she overreacted?

No. She was a new mother.

At the emergency room, they did an X-ray of her son's lungs to determine how polluted they were. They wound up giving him a breathing treatment before sending Beth home with him. They also recommended she follow up with his pediatrician.

After examining her son, reading the report from the emergency room and listening to Beth's concerns, Dr. Smith prescribed a nebulizer with albuterol for her son.

That's how Beth learned about respiratory medicine.

Over the coming weeks and months as Greg and Beth fought to keep their young son alive, Beth learned how to operate her son's nebulizer equipment like a pro. She also became better at properly reading his breathing situation at any given time.

CHAPTER 19

As if Beth didn't have enough stress to deal with; she was still fighting this legal battle with her mother and Pete while learning to care for her new son, a new house and husband. Was this normal? Did everyone have to fight their parents and a bunch of lawyers in court to get their property and basic rights?

Beth was pissed the day she got a phone call from Tad. "I just want to give you a heads up. The court will be sending you documentation reflecting the judge's most recent ruling in this matter. He just awarded sanctions to Pete, your mother and that bank. He's forcing you to pay for their lawyers and all their costs so they can all fight you in court. I'm really sorry, Beth. Pete obviously has some very powerful friends in this town," Tad said dejectedly. Beth still believed justice would prevail in this situation. It just had to. It wasn't right she'd be forced to remain locked in this guardianship for the rest of her life. She was getting really tired of the court robbing her every single month to pay these damn lawyers. They billed her for all kinds of stuff. Every time she turned around another lawyer was picking her pocket. Her dumbass mother!

Beth remembered those years when her mother fought the federal government on her behalf when she was a kid. She remembered the night her mother came home from another battle with the government in the fall of 1992 and announced to Beth she had done it. She had finally settled with the feds.

Her mother assured her that she would be taken care of for the rest of her life. She would never want for anything.

From her mother's perspective, she hadn't wanted for anything. The problem was Beth didn't want that stupid money. She wanted an education and the right to determine her own future—just like any other American. Was that too much to ask?

Beth realized this was her mother's original intention, to set Beth up so she would be able to follow her dreams—no matter what they were. The problem was; all these lawyers were picking her pockets while blocking Beth's access to that money.

That night in 1992 Beth realized this was the answer in her mother's mind—getting all this money. Surely, if the pot was big enough everything would be fine. But Beth wasn't demanding answers from her poor mother. She expected God to make it all right. She didn't want a pot of money. She wanted her abilities back and a chance to live her life on her own terms. If only her mother realized those scheming lawyers only wanted to block Beth from ever getting better so she could take over that pot of money.

They blocked everything God and Beth were trying to do all those years. Just to protect that money. Her mother's plan backfired, and her blind, brain-injured daughter wound up paying the ultimate price for years.

Beth despised those effing lawyers for it all.

Hey, do you want to hear a joke? What do you call a thousand 1,000 dead lawyers at the bottom of the sea? A decent start. LOL! Sorry, just a little survivor humor there. I'm a survivor of guardianship abuse.

CHAPTER 20

Beth's son grew in size and ability. Beth was careful not to block his progress in any way. She knew he might have some struggles. She would just be patient with him and make sure he always had the support he needed in life.

As the months went by Beth's son grew stronger and healthier while his parents hurtled towards this inevitable court hearing with Pete and Beth's mother. The stress Greg and Beth were experiencing was enormous. This is why Beth chose to turn a blind eye to Greg's forgetfulness. Until it started impacting the safety of their baby boy.

The day Beth stepped up onto the sidewalk next to Greg and asked, "Where's the baby?" Beth realized what a moron she married. Greg got out of the car and left the baby strapped into his car seat right behind him.

What made the whole thing worse was Greg loved reminding Beth he had more parenting experience than she did. Well, Beth never forgot the baby anywhere . . . least of all in the backseat of the car!

Beth was pissed, and terrified. This was the man who she was expected to trust her son with? She took to praying fervently for her son every time he was out of her sight if he was in his father's care after that.

Honestly, concern for the safety of her son was all that kept Beth with Greg at first. She knew if she left him, she would have no way of protecting her baby when he was out of her sight and in his father's care. Greg was so absent-minded; he was downright dangerous if Beth left him alone with the baby.

CHAPTER 21

One day, while her baby was napping, Beth was doing laundry and playing with her blind Rat, Micky. Just as Beth was walking by the front door with a basket of laundry in her arms and Mickey perched upon her head, she heard a knock.

Setting the basket of laundry down on the landing Beth asked, "Who is it?"

"It's me, Marjory!" came the reply.

Shit! She should run and put Mickey in his cage before she opened the door. Then, Beth had a better idea. She loved having fun at the expense of all these idiots; now she found their queen standing right outside her front door.

She reached up onto her head, gently stroking Mickey. "Hold on, little guy. I want to introduce you to someone really special."

Then Beth opened her front door with a big old grin plastered across her face, awaiting Marjory's reaction. It was priceless.

"Oh, Beth! That is sooooo inappropriate!" Beth struggled to hide the fact she was laughing her ass off. Stupid bitch!

Beth was fascinated at how afraid Marjory was of one of God's creatures. It was so easy having fun at Marjory's expense. What would happen if she walked into a therapy session or courtroom with Mickey sometime? How would the judge or her therapist react? Mickey was, for all intents and purposes, her emotional support animal.

She knew not only was Mickey blind; he had also sustained a severe brain injury of his own.

Her poor little rat was not only missing one eye, the other one being completely white, he also had severe injuries to his head.

It seemed to Beth when Greg first gave Mickey to her that God had made him just for her. Why was Marjory so repulsed by this innocent, gentle creature?

And why was Beth so eccentric in her thinking? She realized this was probably what enabled her to finally defeat it all. Her ability to think outside the box and be comfortable and not afraid in nearly any situation. It was just those courtrooms and lawyers she feared these days . . . Beth's ability to change her perspective had gotten her out of more than one scrape over the years. Thank God, He enabled her to change her perspective in these ways.

So, you see, a person can learn a lot from a blind rat.

Sadly, when Mickey made his escape from his cage late one night while Beth and Greg lay sleeping; he didn't survive.

Beth bawled her eyes out the next morning when Greg handed her the limp body of her blind, little rat. Mickey somehow got out of his cage and the family cat got ahold of him.

When Greg found him, Mickey was barely clinging to life. The vet who made the house call gave Mickey a mercy shot to put him out of his misery.

Beth was horrified. Would she meet a similar fate if she ever managed to escape from her own cage?

CHAPTER 22

As the months went by Beth wound up reading so much legal shit; she thought about going to law school to round off her legal education. Why not? Someone had to go to war with these disagreeable lawyers, on their own turf. Someone who was smarter than them. Someone who knew all their tricks. Someone who had already outsmarted them. Maybe someday, when she wasn't so busy with all her other projects, she would have time to pursue this line of attack as well. First things first.

Beth made detailed notes on three different depositions that year—Pete's, Marjory's and her mother's.

This experience killed her. These were the three people she thought were on her team. These three in particular knew about her suffering better than anyone. Why would they conspire against her like this?

Beth wiped her tears from the pages as she made her notes. She couldn't let the ink become too smudged. Tad had to be able to read these notes later if they were going to be of any help to her in court.

As Beth prayed for Marjory when she fell off her horse that year, she realized this woman had intentionally set out to hurt her and her family. How could God expect her to pray for this bitch at a time like this?

Beth knew she had been commanded to pray for her enemies. So, she prayed. Heap those coals, Lord!

Was it His way of justifying His actions a short time later when Beth learned Marjory's house caught fire? Was this part of His justice on Beth's behalf? Heaven only knew.

No one was hurt in the fire, thank God. The damage surely impacted Marjory financially though, not to mention stealing her peace from her for a bit. These were the same ways in which Marjory had hurt Beth so deeply. That was some consolation for Beth.

The fire surely depreciated the value of Marjory's antique home as well.

Beth didn't believe in seeking revenge but if God Himself chooses to do something, who was she to argue with His wisdom?

Honestly, Beth could see how they had been conspiring against her from the very beginning. How had Beth missed the signs indicating their true treachery?

Beth always knew in the back of her mind they were out to get her. Playing dumb to them was her best defense all those years. They would have just poisoned her and gotten rid of her if they had any idea she was making herself better on the inside while they tried to destroy the outside.

This fight had made her so very strong, and clever. As a result, Beth was certain she would survive anything they ever tried in the future as well. Bring it on, you sons-of-bitches! It's showtime. Beth was after all "The Measuring Life." She'd been busy measuring for years now. She knew she was far ahead of the rest of them.

CHAPTER 23

When she handed her notes to Tad, he was thrilled. "This is great! Having your thoughts regarding all of this may help me fight for you better."

Beth smiled. She would continue to take an active role in this process.

Beth was chatting with Tad one day when the subject of her stress came up.

"I understand you may hesitate to approach Pete for this Beth but going on a vacation is perfectly reasonable. Why don't you put together a proposed budget and I'll submit it to Pete for his consideration? The worst he can do is say no. And, if he does, it will make him look like a really big jerk when we finally go to court in a few months."

So, Beth and Greg took their son to Silverwood in Idaho for a few days. It was an amazing trip! And not having to deal with Pete's bullshit about how much money she was spending on the trip was also refreshing. That guy acted like he was the one who had suffered and died for that money. This is why Beth shouldn't have been surprised the day she found out Pete had himself put on her life insurance policies as beneficiary.

That's right. This shyster is named on her life insurance policies. The ones from Allstate. The ones she was awarded when she was a minor.

Talk about corruption! How was Beth going to keep Pete from stealing her property from her after all? If she died before she could get this straightened out, Pete and her mother would get everything Beth had been working for and should be allowed to leave to her children. Those crooks! Would this nightmare ever truly be over? Today, almost ten years after Beth finally succeeded in terminating that guardianship, she is only now learning this information.

Beth realized she must be coming to the end of all their treachery, surely. How much could her parents and their lawyers steal from her in one lifetime?

CHAPTER 24

Beth should have recognized it as a sign of things to come. It was the Friday before their court date. Beth was busy reading through more legal shit.

She was using the old, boxy CCTV her parents allowed her to buy right after the lawsuit was settled in 1992—when Beth was just fifteen years old. It was the first machine she was able to read with after the injury. The machine was almost twelve years old by now.

Beth still remembered her joy that day. The day she found something that would allow her to read literally anything she got her hands on—as long as she could stick the pages under her CCTV.

Over the years since that day Beth had read schoolbooks, bulletins from church, legal thrillers, racy romance novels, teen magazines, whatever she could get her hands on. She even enjoyed doing cross-word puzzles to sharpen her mental faculties.

She had been using it to read all this legal shit as well. This is why she shouldn't have been surprised when her CCTV finally gave up the ghost that night.

Beth realized how much she depended on her CCTV that weekend. As she struggled to cope with her anxiety regarding the upcoming court hearing, she could do nothing to prepare herself. Nor could she do any reading for pure enjoyment to take her mind off it all.

By Monday morning, Beth was a nervous wreck.

She prayed silently to herself as she kissed her baby goodbye before she and Greg left for the courthouse.

"Remember, no one is allowed to come in this house while we're gone today, not even friends or family," Beth stressed to her stepdaughter before she and Greg ran out the door.

Beth wasn't taking any chances. She wanted to make sure the kids were safe while they were in court.

CHAPTER 25

Beth felt like she was walking to her own execution as she followed Greg into the courthouse that first morning. She knew all these lawyers were after her blood. Most of them had been feeding on her twitching carcass for over a decade now. They were all counting on her never rising again.

Would her friend Eric make it to testify on her behalf? Beth knew his testimony would be particularly relevant. These assholes were trying to convince the judge she was being held back, that she was "losing her edge." The actual situation was quite different. Eric's testimony would clearly show her true fight for independence. Plus, Eric had known her far longer than even her husband and Marjory. Her friend Eric was in a wheelchair. When Beth first met him, Eric was very antisocial and never went out. Beth could see how weary he had become while living with his own struggles. Over time they became great friends as Beth encouraged and prompted Eric to come out of his shell. Beth was always inviting Eric out for lunch and other activities in public. It was similar to what she did with her other friend Randy when she first met him. Beth was always encouraging Eric to come out of his shell. And it worked! How could she be anti-independence with stories like these on her resume? And these were far from the only ones.

Unfortunately, the weather was too bad in Missoula that January day, and Eric couldn't make the journey down Broadway Avenue in his wheelchair from his home at Eagle Watch to the courthouse.

Beth was fairly certain if the judge heard from Eric—someone else who was living a similar struggle—he would see all the ways in which Beth had been overcoming her disability every single day. Beth had never allowed her disability stop her. It was everyone else's paranoia about her disability that held Beth back. All these lawyers and their cronies only knew and saw what they wanted to see and believe. Beth and Eric were true experts when it came to living with and overcoming a disability.

CHAPTER 26

The first day of testimony was rather uneventful. Just a bunch of professionals and laymen bloviating but on Beth's behalf.

Beth rolled her eyes as she listened to the lawyers from the bank interrogating her closest friends—both personal friends and professional contacts. Those lawyers were obviously obsessed with the money. How would any of these people have a clue about this stuff? It wasn't as if Beth sat around discussing with anyone how much money she had or what she did with it. Pete and the lawyers from the bank were the only people Beth had ever met who even cared about such things.

And boy, did they care about it! To the extent they took Beth's very life from her in order to protect that money.

The only thing the rest of these people knew was their poor friend blind Beth was being abused by the system. Of course, they would go to court and testify for her. And Greg too, if necessary.

Now their friends found themselves being put through this stupidity? Beth was torn up inside as she listened to her pastor being raked over the coals by Pete's attorney. Thank God her pastor was so tough. With his background, Beth knew nothing intimidated him.

When Beth sat in the witness stand, Daniels proved himself a true ass. Beth was shocked when he humiliated her as he made fun of her blindness like that. Beth still wanted to punch that bastard for how he spoke down to her that day—in front of the judge. Beth couldn't believe the judge let that shit go on in his courtroom.

She shouldn't have been surprised. She had been living in this male-dominated, abusive society her entire life. She longed for the day when she would show them all just who this woman was, this woman they had been underestimating.

When Beth was being interrogated by Pete's attorney all she could think was; what was he thinking as he watched his own lawyer; the one Beth was being forced to pay for, trying to rip apart this blind woman; the one he was supposed to be protecting? Was Pete shocked when he saw her up there on the stand, testifying against him like that? Beth knew this asshole was the one who silenced her all those years they fought the lawsuit—the years they locked her down and robbed her of an education and hope.

Beth was amused as Pete's lawyer tried to justify all the shit Pete and Marjory had done to her. Surely, she realized they were only doing what was in her best interest . . .

She had been plotting her revenge for decades now. How could anyone decide to steal a little girl's entire life from her like they did? She managed to take it back, only to have them steal it again when she was just twenty. She just had to escape.

CHAPTER 27

Beth watched helplessly as the attorneys from the other side crucified Greg on cross-examination. Beth already figured out how to get out of this trap. What right did they have to judge her lifestyle choices?

Too bad she never managed to help Greg understand this concept.

Tears streamed down Beth's cheeks when she watched as they first put Greg on the defensive about little things before springing their big trap once he was stressed out and off-balance. Greg walked right into their trap.

Beth almost burst out laughing when she first heard their ridiculous accusations towards her husband. These idiots actually thought he was an active member of the local homosexual community and had been hanging out at the local gay bar in town writing personal checks! This was way out there, even for Pete. It must be his new lawyer who gave him that stupid idea.

Of course, it was all a load of hogwash, but by then Greg just looked guilty as hell of whatever they decided to pin on him. Beth was guilty by association. Talk about a kangaroo court! No evidence required here. Have you heard any rumors, partner?

The really funny thing was Greg was for all intents and purposes impudent. Beth barely tolerated it during their marriage. She was certain none of the gay men around town would stand for it. Pete and his stupid ideas again. Beth thought attorneys did their research . . .?

At the end of the first day, Beth still felt confident.

CHAPTER 28

The next morning Beth and Greg stood in the lobby of the courthouse visiting with Tad and his associate while they waited for their hearing to resume.

Suddenly Beth realized Pete was probably lurking nearby, waiting also. Where was he? Her blood ran cold when she realized he was standing just across the lobby with his attorney and those from the bank.

What was he thinking as he watched her chatting and cutting up with her attorneys? Was he regretful for the relationship he never bothered to cultivate with her those years when he had the opportunity? He could have done so much for her; had he only cared enough to get to know her like these other guys had.

Pete's attorney had the balls to get up first thing that second morning after court came to order.

Beth couldn't believe it when that bastard motioned the court to dismiss her entire case to terminate the guardianship.

Beth smiled when the judge informed that asshole there was plenty of prima facie for terminating the guardianship; her case would be heard.

Beth hung on every word as Pete's attorney tried to explain away his client's gross overbilling of his blind client that came to light the day before.

As Pete bragged about this overwhelming and very expensive network of people he hired to "take care" of his ward since he was so far away, Beth started to realize just how much of her property this guy squandered in the name of protecting her from herself.

She realized she would be lucky if she had anything left when she finally won this case; the way all these judges and lawyers were always spending her money and handing it out to everyone but her.

Beth resented it when Pete sat there listing off all the stuff "the trust" had been providing to her as if she owed them something for letting her live in this house, the one they forced her to buy and then locked her in.

She was absolutely appalled as Pete sat there describing his version of the courtship between her and Greg. This guy was so disconnected from her life; how could he possibly have a clue what he was talking about? No wonder he had become so paranoid whenever Beth was forced to talk to him. He was only getting bad information, and this came directly from Marjory. Beth was already aware of Marjory's agenda.

When she listened to those stupid neuropsychologists, Beth was so angry she could scream. Why did they think she demonstrated all those behavior problems and "personality defects" back when she was a teenager? Could it have anything to do with the fact her brain was struggling through adolescence and this after sustaining a major brain injury that had gone untreated; not to mention the cocktail of chemicals they were pouring into her scrambled brains back then. What else did they expect from her? They were just lucky she hadn't gone postal on them.

Beth tried not to laugh out loud when Greg whispered in her ear about Dr. Johnson's stupid getup when he was on the stand. That idiot with the swollen head had obviously gone out of his way to doll himself up for his debut appearance as an "expert "witness in this sham of a trial.

Beth sighed. She realized she was dealing with a bunch of Neanderthals.

Beth almost fell out of her chair when she realized her attorney was showing the world Dr. Johnson had misdiagnosed her brain injury all those years. This idiot was treating her for a frontal lobe injury when everyone else knew the tumor was located in the rear hemisphere of the brain. No wonder Beth hated seeing him. She always felt terrible when she left Dr. Johnson's office those years when Pete was forcing her to go see him. Well, if he was tweaking her brain the wrong way because he was confused about what her injuries were, it was no wonder. What a bunch of stupid people she was dealing with here!

More ridiculous yet, this stupid idiot was one of the "experts" her mother's lawyers relied upon when they screwed the federal government. Now, Beth finds out the guy was totally clueless from the very beginning!

All she could do was hide her face in humiliation as Dr. Johnson recounted the stupid "team" meetings they forced her and Greg to sit through while these other people argued all the reasons why they should or shouldn't be married. How stupid was that? Beth was still miffed the court had made her come to them, her hat in hand, begging them to let her get married when she was twenty-four years old.

After the journey to get that far, was it any wonder Beth hesitated to try getting out of the marriage initially? She knew it would be another big battle with these idiots, one that would cost her any chance of ever escaping from this guardianship.

When Beth found out she was pregnant, one of her first thoughts was, oops, I forgot to get permission to have sex.

Johnson's shit didn't help Beth either. He needed to learn how to properly understand his patients, the idiot. With no one on her side, what was she to do?

As Johnson shared his opinion that Beth was totally inept, Beth wanted to share her opinion with him as well. Her opinion was that none of these so-called "experts" could prove anything they were saying because it was all pure conjecture on their part. Beth was literally the only person who was standing at such a vantage point her perspective enabled her to see what was on the inside, the outside, the past, present and future. The day Beth fully realized this, she knew she was on the right track—no matter what those stupid doctors and experts said.

Beth wanted to laugh as she listened to Pete describe why he figured Dr. Johnson should have had more of a hand in helping her understand how to be a proper wife. Did this mean Pete wanted this stupid doctor to coach her on her oral techniques in the bedroom? That's what it sounded like to Beth's ears!

As Beth listened to Pete describe the process surrounding the prenup, she realized what they were worried about. Beth didn't sign her prenup on her own behalf, Pete did. If she managed to nullify the guardianship it would automatically void their precious prenup, thus, putting Beth's estate in jeopardy. Thanks again, Mom.

As Beth listened to Pete describe how he felt when she became pregnant, she remembered how scared she was all those months. Pete was such a loose cannon, and he had all her rights. She was just waiting for someone to show up at her front door to drag her away for a forced abortion at his behest. She knew Pete was totally freaked out about her pregnancy. Beth always wondered what happened to her right to choose what happened to her own body?

Finally, her mother took the stand.

CHAPTER 29

As her mother talked about all the reasons she thought Pete had done a fine job as her disabled daughter's full-guardian, all Beth could think about was that these two thieves had gotten their names put on her life insurance policies from Allstate. Talk about a conflict of interest! Why couldn't this stupid judge see this?

As she listened to her mother whine about stuff she didn't entirely understand about her adult daughter's life, Beth was incensed. This stupid court was going to allow this unstable, disturbed woman who had never accepted her daughter survived, to dictate that same daughter's future?

Her mentally ill mother was clueless about how far Beth had come on this journey towards independence.

Her mother's appearance in the courtroom that evening had the desired effect on Beth. She played right into Pete's scheming mitts on this one.

Beth realized too late they set her up to already be an emotional mess when Pete's girlfriend Marjory took the stand to finish her off.

Beth couldn't believe it when her mother actually had the balls to ask Beth if she could "stop by the house to see her grandson before she left town?"

"Of course not! Stay away from us. You're not welcome in our presence anymore," was how Beth and her mother parted that day; the day Beth realized her mother believed more in that money than she did her own daughter.

When Marjory took the stand, Beth listened as she spun a wild tale. It was a story about everything she had allegedly been told by all her friends, the ones Greg and Beth were forced to allow in their home. The hearsay that was entered into evidence that day was outrageous. Beth just couldn't believe this corrupt excuse for a court of law. Beth was never given a chance for rebuttal witnesses so she could reveal all their lies that day.

This is why Beth shouldn't have been surprised when the judge ruled against her a short time later.

Beth first listened as His Honor spoke about how intelligent she was; she could match wits with anyone else in the courtroom.

Alas, what about all these vicious rumors? What if they were true?

Well, better safe than sorry. So, that stupid judge refused to set Beth free that day.

CHAPTER 30

Beth cried for weeks. She couldn't be comforted. Even her sleep at night was disrupted. How could that judge do this to her? Beth knew now she really wasn't incapacitated. This meant there was only one answer; the system must be broken. She would simply figure out how to fix it.

Beth started studying the law. Well, she had already been studying the law for years while battling these dumb lawyers. She just became more focused on what she was doing. Before, it was more of a pastime, trying to figure out how to get out of this guardianship. It had suddenly become of utmost importance.

The first document Beth read when she was finally able to replace her broken CCTV was the Constitution of the United States of America. Starting at the beginning always seemed best to Beth.

As Beth read the preamble to this divinely inspired document, these words spoke to her on a level no other document ever had—except the Word of God. She knew with certainty these words were written for her.

As she read the words "All men were created equally by God and have been endowed with certain unalienable rights," Beth was struck with the idea that these words surely applied to her also.

As she continued to read further, she was struck that each of the protections that were guaranteed to all Americans had been denied her at one point or another during all these years she'd been locked down under this guardianship.

When Beth realized the entire state of Montana had violated her constitutional rights, she was livid. Beth found the legal dynamite she would use to blow the doors off her own guardianship and eventually these corrupt, broken laws that day. She would free everyone from these oppressive cages forever.

CHAPTER 31

When Beth went back to court on January 25th, 2012, she set a legal precedent that day when she demanded the state of Montana recognize that she was a human being, entitled to the same rights and protections guaranteed to everyone else. Furthermore, she demanded they release her immediately on these grounds.

If you are locked under your own court-appointed guardianship or conservatorship, you can do the same. You have the power inside of you also.

Terminating her own guardianship was only the beginning. Beth's mission became to terminate the very legal ordinances that were written into the guardianship laws. They needed to be rewritten to protect others.

Beth knew now why He had been randomly crossing her path with other victims of guardianship abuse over the years. He wanted to show her she wasn't only fighting for herself, but for each of these others as well.

Beth was shocked when she realized the powerful position He had brought her to in order to lodge this attack on the guardianship laws.

This is how He showed Beth what His plan was for her life in such a big way even a blind woman couldn't miss it. The pieces were all falling into place.

The only way to do this right was to go to the top and take those laws down at the legislative level.

Hmmmm . . . Beth goes to Congress?

That's right! Beth feels the calling to go fight these laws and take them out from the top down. She plans to rewrite the guardianship laws so they will actually protect people.

Beth knew better than anyone else the power of the written word. She just had to figure out how to wield it for her victory in court next time—and there would be a next time. Beth didn't roll over for anyone, least of all a bunch of unscrupulous effing lawyers.

Once she got her feet under her, she took care of that tumor. Now, it was time to do the same to this new monster.

AFTERWORD

On January 25, 2012, Beth walked out of court victorious over that legal monster. It got the court's attention when her attorney pointed out his client's constitutional rights had been violated by the administration of this guardianship. The judge couldn't cut Beth loose fast enough that day.

In August 2019 Beth opened her company Blue Butterfly Enterprises where she has been building her own improvised explosive device she will use to take out these corrupt, broken laws forever. This is the only way to free us all at once, my friends. We are each in danger of this happening to us the way the laws are currently written.

Sincerely yours,
Rebecca Meadows: Guardianship Slayer Extraordinaire
Founder and CEO of Blue Butterfly Enterprises LLC and host and creator of Becca's World on YouTube

GRETCH THE WRETCH

CHAPTER 1

Gretchen Stone hummed to herself as she walked with the flow of traffic through the Las Vegas airport, casually swinging her long, white cane from side to side.

It felt good to stretch her legs. She couldn't wait to get to the hotel where she could get settled.

When the other passengers from her flight reached their baggage claim, Gretch stood back for a few moments.

This was her first trip to Las Vegas; she didn't know a soul in Nevada. She had come to attend her first National Federation of the Blind annual convention.

First, she had to find her suitcase. Then she would make her way down to ground transportation where she could catch a ride to the hotel.

Gretch jumped when she heard a loud alarm. With a sudden jerk, the conveyor belt began to move.

She heard the unmistakable thuds of bags landing on the conveyor belt behind the wall.

As the belt continued to move, Gretch was aware of other passengers standing around, chatting with each other.

People began stepping forward, grabbing their suitcases from the moving belt.

It wasn't long before a young man approached, suggesting he might assist her in finding her bag. Gretch smiled and gratefully accepted his offered help.

She quickly gave him a detailed description of her suitcase, right down to the big, beautiful, blue butterfly sticker she had affixed to one side.

She added with a sly wink, "You'd have to be blind to miss it!"

The kind stranger laughed right out loud as he strolled away in search of her bag.

Gretch was still chuckling a few minutes later when she reached into her purse to find her iPhone. Pulling it from her bag, she pressed the side button, powering it on. She quickly created a text to her roommate back in Mesa letting him know she had arrived in Nevada safely.

As Gretchen sat there catching her breath, she thought about all the fun she was bound to have this week.

Gretch totally embraced the NFB's philosophy on life. "Blind people can do anything; blindness isn't what holds us back!"

She knew her own life's experience was proof of this.

Gretch was pulled from her musings a few minutes later when the young man reappeared, towing both their bags behind him. He smiled and said, "Can I help you with anything else?"

"Thank you for retrieving my bag. Can you give me directions to ground transportation where I can request a Lyft, please?"

"Sure. Just take a left at the end of that hallway over there and follow the rideshare signs until you're outside. You can't miss it!"

Gretch struggled to hold back her laughter as she held up her white cane in one hand, reminding him about her blindness.

The man laughed at himself and remarked, "Oh, sorry! I guess I forgot already."

"Don't feel bad. I forget every single day."

Then she added, "Can you just give me directions to the hallway you mentioned? I bet I can find my way from there."

After the man gave her the directions Gretch set out, tapping her cane in her right hand while towing her suitcase behind her with her left.

After walking quite a distance she felt a slight breeze on her face, alerting her she was approaching an exterior doorway.

Gretch confidently stepped through the opening, relieved to feel the sunshine and rush of fresh air on her face.

She quickly took inventory of her surroundings. She heard distant traffic sounds on her right side and very little noise on the other. That must be the tarmac, Gretch thought to herself.

As she confidently turned to the right, she realized there was a curb several yards away. She gingerly headed in that direction, tapping her cane all the way.

When she approached, she caught a glimpse of a man in a bright orange vest as he moved back and forth, monitoring the traffic as the cars raced through the airport access road.

She approached him, asking if he could help her keep an eye out for her ride.

"Sure. What car are you waiting for?"

Because it was so hard to hear out there that close to the tarmac, she simply held up her iPhone, letting the man read the information directly off her Lyft app.

"Got it! I'll let you know when he gets here."

Gretch smiled at him as she relaxed on a nearby bench, reaching into her purse to remove her vape pen.

As she sat there puffing on her vape, she thought about how much she loved her life. She almost felt guilty for being so happy. It just didn't seem right somehow . . .

She knew her mother was still out there somewhere, suffering. What entitled Gretch to this life?

She was so thankful her mother had finally seen fit to set her free to live her life on her own terms.

Did that life really have to be one without her mother in it?

Gretch still prayed for her mother every single day. Her heart's desire was to see her mom again someday.

Maybe one day she'd finally figure out how to make things right. For the next few days at least, she had a convention to experience!

CHAPTER 2

When her car finally arrived, the traffic monitor loaded her suitcase in the trunk while Gretch climbed into the front seat, fastening her seatbelt across her body. She leaned forward, placing her water bottle and purse between her feet on the floor.

She smiled at the driver, asking him how his day was.

As he wove his way through the city traffic towards Flamingo Boulevard, he asked her what was going on." I've been picking up people like you for two days and taking all of them to that place on Flamingo. They've been coming by bus, plane and train. I even picked up this guy and his guide dog at the truck stop who hitched a ride into town with an over-the-road trucker. I just dropped them off at the hotel about an hour ago."

Gretch wasn't surprised. She knew her blind peers to be very resourceful individuals when they put their minds to a project. Of course, they would find a way to make it to the NFB national convention.

"You know, it's a good thing I met you. I actually have a neighbor who is dealing with recent vision loss. I watch him stumble out to get his garbage can from the street every week. He occasionally trips over the curb. I've noticed he doesn't leave his house by himself anymore either."

"Oh, that poor man! All he needs is a little training and he could live a successful life on his own terms. I hope he gets connected with the NFB."

She began telling the man about all the wonderful stuff she had gleaned from her affiliation with the group.

As they pulled up to the hotel, she advised him to go to NFB.org to get more information. The man quickly jotted the information down as he climbed out of the car to retrieve her suitcase from the trunk.

"Thank you for your help, sir."

"No, thank you! I can't wait to talk to my neighbor. I think the NFB may be just what he needs."

"If he takes their advice and embraces the long, white cane and is willing to learn his blind immersion skills, there is absolutely no reason he can't enjoy a very successful life. He can even go back to work, or school if he likes. It just takes finding the right people to give him the proper training."

As the man pulled away from the curb, Gretch made her way through the front door of the hotel.

The uproar in the lobby was insane!

There were people everywhere. Most of them blind, all tapping their canes or using their guide dogs as they maneuvered through the unfamiliar lobby. It took Gretchen's breath away.

It took a lot of finesse for her to make her way through the crowd without stepping on a dog paw or tail.

Gretch finally found herself at the front of the group, facing the front desk clerk.

She reached into her purse, removing her wallet.

As she flipped it open, she casually slid her finger across the top and down the right side where she kept her cards.

She counted down until she felt the third slot, her credit card. She promptly removed it.

She skillfully slid her ID card out of its designated pocket as well.

After sticking her wallet back in her purse, she turned to the desk clerk, handing him her cards.

"Thank you, MS. Stone. We have you registered in a double queen room for five nights, charged at the special NFB convention rate. Would you like your room keys? I can have the bellman show you to your room when he walks your luggage up."

"Thank you, that would be nice." Gretch turned from the desk, following the bellman as he headed for the elevators with her luggage.

Being an outgoing, friendly person Gretch engaged the bellman in conversation as they made their way up to her floor.

As they exited the elevator, Gretch noted the low hum of a soft drink machine in a utility room as they wound their way down the hall towards her room.

She took the envelope containing her room keys from her purse. Removing one, she held it up, inspecting both sides. As usual, she couldn't decern anything significant on either side.

Oh well! I lose again, she thought to herself. She had become accustomed to being disappointed in these matters over the years. By now, it just came with the territory. Maybe someday life would become truly and fully accessible to someone like her . . .

Turning to the bellman, she asked him to help her.

After he aided her in positioning the card properly, she asked him to notch the very tip of the top righthand corner with something sharp so she would know how to orient it in her hand for future use.

Once they were inside her room, Gretch asked the bellman to adjust the room thermostat to a comfortable temperature. She had him make sure the blinds were covering the windows completely so no one would be able to see in later.

She also asked him to help her find an electrical outlet near the nightstand where she could plug in her multi-outlet power strip.

After giving the bellman a fair tip for all his hospitality, Gretch saw him to the door.

"I almost forgot. Do you know if the front desk has small refrigerators for rent?"

"Yes, ma'am. Would you like me to bring one to your room?"

Gretch thought about it for a moment before asking," Is there a charge for the fridge?"

"Normally yes, but as a perk of being here with the NFB, the fee is being waived this week. Would you like me to bring one up for you?"

"That would be nice. Thanks for the information."

"Anytime. We've been very excited to host your group's convention."

After she closed the door, she returned to the bedroom.

Gretch spent the next hour unpacking her suitcase. She unfolded each of her dresses, hanging them in the closet. She neatly folded and organized her undergarments in the dresser as well.

She put her toiletries away in the bathroom.

When she got to the bottom of her suitcase, she ran her hand across the synthetic material, checking to see if she had left anything behind.

She was confused when she heard a metallic clink. When she took a closer look at what was in her suitcase she was horrified.

Gretch held up four hollow, metal bars in one hand and a frayed, elastic strap in the other. It was the remains of her folding cane—the one she always carried with her for emergencies when she traveled away from home.

Someone had murdered this invaluable companion of hers.

It could be only one person. She had found his calling card when she first opened her suitcase. It was an effing TSA agent!

What would she do if she broke her long, white cane? She knew the chances of that happening here at the convention were far more likely than any of the other places she traveled. She would be helpless.

Gretch never wanted to be helpless ever again.

Gretch enjoyed traveling whenever she could. As a result, she had experienced her share of TSA's stupid antics.

They became all thumbs when they saw her approaching their checkpoints at her home airport. She never knew what bad experience she was going to have with a TSA agent next. They were uncouth and made a habit of doing stupid stuff like wrenching her cane from her hand before rudely nudging her towards the device they wanted her to walk through. They never used common courtesy or basic language to communicate with her. It was stupid.

They almost always chose her for the "random" pat-downs as if a terrorist would choose to pose as a harmless blind woman to evade discovery.

Gretch knew there was one big problem with this ignorant theory. Blind people were far from harmless.

It had been Gretchen's experience that it was only fools and lawyers who underestimated the abilities of a blind woman.

(She had grown weary of them placing their filthy hands on her body just so they could cop a cheap feel.)

On another occasion, she was separated from her two small children when an ignorant TSA agent just grabbed her by the arm and rudely dragged her away from her two little boys and left them standing there all alone in the TSA line. As that agent led her around the corner out of sight of the public all Gretch could think about was the reports she had heard of innocent women being taken behind closed doors and gang-raped by TSA agents. She was terrified not only for her own safety but for the safety of her children as well.

Now TSA had left her without her extra cane. She was livid. What was she going to do if she somehow broke her long, white cane? That effing TSA . . .

She had to calm down. Finding her brush, she sat on the edge of the bed. She ran it through her long, bouncy locks, smoothing out the damage the wind had done to them on her way into town.

She removed her CPAP machine from its case, plugging it into the surge protector after setting it on the nightstand. After connecting the hose to the machine, she neatly folded her nightgown and put it on her Sleep Number pillow.

She also plugged in her cell phone charger, her vape charger and Victor Reader Trek. She wanted everything to be ready when she went to bed later.

Gretch suddenly realized she forgot to stop at a convenience store on her way from the airport.

Crap! She had to find a way to get distilled water for her CPAP sometime yet today.

She reached over, picking up the room phone on the nightstand.

As she listened to the dial tone, she expertly ran her fingertips across and down the front of the phone, making a quick study of the panel of buttons.

Locating the number zero, she pressed it, holding her breath.

When a cheery voice answered, Gretch asked if there was a gift shop in the lobby.

"Yes, I'll connect you now," came the staticky response.

As Gretch sat there praying she wouldn't get disconnected, she found herself yawning. It had been a long day. The trip just getting here was an adventure . . .

When the lady at the gift shop picked up the phone, Gretch asked if she had distilled water.

"Yes."

"Great! Can you give me directions to your shop from the elevator door in the lobby please?"

After getting the needed information from the woman, Gretch hung up and ran to the bathroom.

She gargled with minty fresh mouthwash before quickly applying fresh deodorant to her underarms and spraying a spritz of perfume under her chin.

Then she grabbed her purse and cane and ran out the door. It was time to go have a look around downstairs.

CHAPTER 3

When the elevator doors slid open, it sounded like a dog show! The chaos hadn't subsided since her earlier visit to the lobby. If anything; it had become even more chaotic. She had to get this water just so she could sleep tonight though.

As Gretch cautiously made her way through the boisterous crowd, she found herself struggling to avoid getting backed into or stumbled over by everyone else.

She had almost reached her destination when she suddenly heard loud laughter nearby, just before someone roughly stumbled into her, sending her sprawling.

"Whoops!" came the voice of a woman sounding like she had already had more than enough to drink.

Gretch was recovering from the sudden shock. She wasn't surprised; this was a blind convention after all.

Gretch felt put out when she realized the woman was fully sighted. How rude!

In the next moment, Gretch felt a hand on her shoulder and heard a friendly voice ask if she would like some assistance.

She turned to find a smiling UPS volunteer offering her his arm. As Gretch gratefully accepted his arm, she asked him to help her find the gift shop.

"Oh, you were so close!" the kindly man said as he led her through the rowdy crowd.

She gratefully thanked him when he left her at the entrance to the gift shop a few minutes later.

Along with her distilled water, Gretch grabbed snacks and a case of bottled water. After asking the girl at the cash register to have a bell-man deliver her purchases to her room, Gretch left the gift shop.

As Gretch made her way through the crowd, it wasn't long before the woman from earlier fell into step beside her once again.

Gretch was trying not to encourage the woman when she suddenly invited her up to her room for a party.

Whoa, thought Gretch to herself! Just who is this woman and why is she so interested in me?

When Gretch found out the woman was there celebrating life with a blind friend from college, she felt more comfortable at the prospect of accompanying the entire party up to the penthouse for a celebration.

Surely, she was safe? Well, you only live once and she had already missed out on a lot of it. She had to catch up on life before life left her behind.

After stopping in her room to put her purchases away, Gretch made her way up to the penthouse.

As Gretch mingled in Trudy's suite she met several people—many of them blind, all of them awesome.

She realized her new friend had terrible boundaries as she listened to Trudy prattle on and on about her personal life.

As she listened, Gretch realized her new friend had led an incredibly bizarre life—similar to herself.

Gretch suddenly found herself standing alone while Trudy was having a private phone conversation nearby.

Gretch quickly started to move away to give Trudy privacy, this was her suite after all.

Gretch was horrified when she heard a male voice ask, "Oh! Who was that?" with a carnal hunger in his husky voice as she was slinking away in the other direction.

Crap! She thought to herself. It was obviously a video chat and this guy had caught a glimpse of her. Time to make like a tree and . . .

"Oh, that's my new friend I met in the lobby this evening, son. Her name is Gretch."

"Oh, that pink bow she's wearing in her hair and those doe eyes! She's breathtaking. I have to speak to her! Please, mother?"

By now Gretch was really feeling swept off her feet. She hadn't even realized her hair bow was pink.

What was going on in her life? She had to get away before she got caught in a trap. She knew she would be safe alone in her room.

After she told Trudy and the rest of the gang good night, she stepped out into the hallway, shutting the door firmly behind her.

CHAPTER 4

Now, where was that elevator?

She should have paid more attention earlier when she first made her way up here . . .

After listening for a few moments Gretch took off in search of the elevator. She walked up one hallway and down another before she stopped to listen again. She turned a corner and found herself suddenly standing near an opening. She cautiously stepped through it. She heard a door slide shut behind her.

Gretch realized she had stepped into some kind of maintenance elevator.

As Gretch felt around on the walls in the darkness searching for a button, the elevator suddenly began a rapid descent.

"Oh, shit!" Gretch cursed under her breath. She just wanted to go to her room and go to bed. Where was this elevator taking her?

After a few moments, the elevator stopped with a sudden jolt. Gretch was relieved when the doors slid open.

She cautiously stepped out into the shadowy gloom.

She could feel cool air on her face and hear the muffled sounds of distant traffic. She realized she must be in the underground parking garage that was attached to the hotel.

Shit! It might take her all night to find her way back up to her hotel room.

Gretch really started to panic when she realized no one knew where she was. She was in an unfamiliar area. All by herself. In the dark. She could feel herself beginning to panic . . .

After she took a hit on her vape and got a grip on herself, she reminded herself to stay calm. She knew she had good cane skills and was in a public area. There were no grizzlies or lawyers out there. All she had to do was find her way out of this.

The traffic sounds were coming from above her and off to the right. She headed in that direction, careful that she was using good cane technique so she wouldn't stumble on curbs, vehicles or any other hidden obstacles in the obscure darkness.

She made her way up a wide, steep, curving ramp toward the traffic sounds.

As Gretch reached the top of the ramp she turned, stepping onto the sidewalk.

Keeping the traffic on her parallel side, Gretch made her way along the sidewalk in front of the building until she turned, making her way through the front door of the hotel a few minutes later. She was relieved to feel the artificially cooled air on her sweaty brow as she emerged back into the lobby. She made her way up to her room.

By the time she got there, she was exhausted. Gretch went to bed.

CHAPTER 5

The next morning, Gretch met up with a young friend from the Treasure State affiliate for breakfast.

She was listening with empathetic ears as Eddy told her about what had happened to him in the lobby the night before.

". . . I was coming out of a restaurant, using my cane and carrying my tray of food with the other hand when this guy just came out of nowhere. We ran into each other. What a mess! I lost my dinner in the process."

"And your appetite, I bet. That must have been terrible."

Gretch understood her friend's frustration. She had only narrowly avoided having similar experiences in the lobby herself, and she was partially sighted. She could only imagine the frustration her totally blind peers were dealing with.

"I understand, Eddie. It's because the NFB has invited so many blind people into this confined space. Many of them have had little to no formal O and M training. It's the makings of a disaster if you ask me."

Gretch was so frustrated with the NFB. Even a novice such as herself could see the golden opportunity here.

Why not offer competent, basic O and M training at the conventions each year? Everyone knew gaining access to this valuable training was a huge obstacle for many blind Americans.

The NFB was always encouraging people to embrace their long, white canes. Why not teach people to use them correctly while they had the attention of the users? Everyone knew it was difficult to get into any one of the NFB training centers.

Offering a course like this at the state and national conventions each year would help bridge the gap.

And why not teach introduction to hardcopy braille and ADL skills while they were at it?

Providing these classes would go a long way towards enhancing the safety, security and independence of the nation's blind.

Only the NFB was big enough to tackle a project like this.

Gretch knew for a fact there were braille and O and M instructors in the federation; she had inadvertently met more than her share of them over time.

They had seminars on everything else. Why not at least teach some basic orientation and mobility theory while they were at it?

Oh well, bureaucracies! What's a blind woman to do? One would almost have to publish a book just to get their point across . . .

Eddie was excitedly telling Gretch about the "Rookie Roundup" he had attended. "We all met together so they could go over some features of the hotel and such. It was fun and interesting."

Gretch was having a great time, no matter what she was doing. There was so much to experience that she had never dreamed of.

"Do you want to go to the general session now?"

"Sure. That would be nice. I have to go get my cell phone from my room first; I left it plugged in. Then I have to park my dog."

"Okay. I think there is a spot along the route to the convention center with access to a dog relief path, isn't there?"

"Yes. I'll catch up with you later. Save me a seat in the convention hall if you make it before me. I'll be along shortly."

Gretch chuckled. She was well aware of how totally dependent everyone was on their technology. This handicap certainly didn't start or end with the blind community. Gretch knew it was only after she had found and learned to use accessible technology that she really started excelling in life. Thank God for the NFB and their training centers!

Gretch grabbed her cane and headed for the seminar while her friend took off in the other direction.

Gretch was relieved there were talking signs along the route to guide her. Each time she was about to give up and turn back, thinking she was heading in the wrong direction, she would hear another talking sign in the distance.

What a cool idea, she thought to herself as she continued along the corridor.

It was quite a hike down to the convention hall from the hotel. She came upon people from various affiliates along the way. Many of them were calling out to convention attendees as they passed by, advertising whatever their individual chapters or affiliates had brought to the convention for fundraisers.

Gretch greeted several friends along the way, recognizing each of them by their voices as they all chatted and laughed with each other. She made many new friends along the way as well.

The blind community was such a friendly, diverse group. The camaraderie was downright nourishing to the soul.

She bought a cloth bag with drawstrings that had the NFB logo on it from a couple of girls sitting at a table. She knew she could use it to carry her souvenirs, no matter how many she wound up collecting.

She purchased stickers supporting the NFB from someone representing another chapter of the federation.

She bought a couple of bottles of cold water from another affiliate. She could use one to refill her insulated flask when it ran low.

Gretch stopped and bought beef sticks from the Treasure State affiliate. When she found someone selling candy bars, she bought a couple for later. She knew she would need something to snack on when she became hungry during the afternoon session.

Many different people were selling a variety of useful products, all in support of the National Federation of the Blind.

When Gretch finally made it to the convention hall, she asked one of the sighted volunteers to keep an eye out for Eddie. "He'll be coming along shortly with his beautiful black guide dog. Can you just point him to where I'm sitting when he arrives, please?"

She was listening to one of the speakers with rapt attention a few minutes later when Eddie suddenly appeared, wanting to sit beside her.

As Gretch slid over to make room for her friend, she took the opportunity to bend over and pet his guide dog, Babe, on the head as she lay on the floor at their feet.

"What are they talking about?" he whispered in her ear.

Gretch handed him a candy bar, one of the beef sticks and the other bottle of cold water.

"They're discussing the legislative agenda of the NFB. These are the issues the NFB will tackle in the next congressional term to make the lives of blind Americans better."

Gretch was so proud to be a member of the NFB. She knew many of their legislative endeavors had the potential of making a difference in the lives of all people, not just blind Americans.

"Thanks for the water and the snack. It will help tide me over until we break for lunch."

"No problem."

The morning session moved along quickly until suddenly the group was breaking up for lunch.

"Come get your prepackaged lunches over here if you signed up for one when you registered," she heard someone call from the back of the room.

"Hi. Did you request a vegetarian meal?" the volunteer asked her as she approached.

"I ordered the chicken salad sandwich. I think I should also be getting a bottle of water with my meal?"

"Yes, just ask one of the volunteers behind you to give you one," he said as he handed her a box lunch with a napkin.

After Gretch got her drink, she turned and made her way back through the crowd to find somewhere to sit and eat.

She found a spot with several other convention attendees sitting around visiting as they ate their lunches.

Gretch unscrewed the lid of her heavy-duty, insulated water flask, balancing it between her legs. She opened the lid of the disposable plastic bottle, resting the open mouth of the plastic bottle against the edge of her thermos. Tilting the bottle up, she dumped its contents into her water jug.

Gretch got a faraway look in her eyes as she focused on what her magic finger eye was seeing when she slyly slid the top portion of her left index finger into the open mouth of her water jug.

Gretch waited to feel the water level rise to the top before lifting the plastic bottle, screwing the lid and straw down tightly.

As Gretch munched on her potato chips, she listened to the folks around her laughing and teasing one another.

Everyone was so relaxed; it felt good to be among such friendly, positive people.

Gretch looked up and smiled when Davis, one of the leaders in the federation stopped to chat with her.

"Hi there. I know you are an ambitious, outgoing young lady. Are you aware we are having a job fair here at the convention this year?"

"No, I had no idea. Thanks for letting me know. I'll spread the word and check it out."

As Davis turned away, she could hear other members vying for his attention. He was very popular among the community. Davis had proven himself to be truly interested in the success and welfare of the blind community.

Gretch had been around. She could see how much thought and effort Davis put in on behalf of the blind community. It was heart-warming to behold.

In the afternoon session, a young woman got up to share her experiences in public school as a blind child.

She had the rapt attention of the entire audience as she described how it felt being unable to participate with the other kids.

"I couldn't read the textbooks or mark my papers without a great deal of difficulty. This made learning nearly impossible. I wasn't allowed to use a cane anywhere. I was falling down the stairs at school all the time and having lots of other accidents everywhere else. Not surprisingly, none of the other students wanted to invite me to do anything after school. I was a huge liability to anyone who chose to be my friend. So, they just didn't choose me."

Gretch, like so many others in the audience, could empathize with the woman totally.

"All this the public school system did to me; a little girl who wanted to be a teacher when she grew up. The day I graduated from that public high school, I couldn't use a computer proficiently, read or write or even cross a city street to get to the other side safely."

She talked about what it felt like being left out of parties, basketball games and other afterschool activities because she didn't have any friends.

She struggled to describe what it was like falling down the stairs at school all the time and how embarrassing it was picking herself up off of the floor and trying to keep from crying as other students and teachers just stood around her—staring and whispering.

"I couldn't compete at the same level as the other students. No one in school wanted to be friends with the blind girl who was a liability." She described how she had been left behind academically because her small-town school district wasn't equipped to accommodate their first blind student ever.

Gretchen wasn't the only person in the room who was wiping tears away as they listened to the young woman's words. The woman wrapped up her presentation by declaring,

"We can't allow another blind child to slip through the cracks of our broken public education system!"

Amen! Gretch thought as she got up to stretch her legs.

CHAPTER 6

Gretchen casually walked out into the hallway to have a look around.

As she mingled in the corridor, she listened to the sounds of other people enjoying the convention around her.

"Get your tickets over here! That's right, step right up."

"What are the tickets for?" she asked as she approached the guy with the big voice.

"These are tickets for tonight's amateur comedy show being put on by one of the affiliates. You can get one ticket for six dollars or two for ten."

"Great! I'll take two tickets, please."

"Here are your tickets. That will be $10, please."

Reaching into her pocket, Gretch pulled out a wad of fives she had. Peeling two of them off she turned, handing them to the guy.

"Thank you. Please enjoy the show!"

Gretch turned away, looking for Eddie in the crowd. When she found him, she asked him if he wanted to have dinner together.

"Sure," he said.

"And then . . . how about you and Babe join me for this amateur comedy show I just bought tickets for?"

"That sounds nice. Thanks for inviting me to join you."

"No problem. It's great seeing you again! I miss my peeps from the Treasure State affiliate. They don't build blind people like they build 'em up in Big Sky Country!" Gretch said with a sardonic laugh.

She was well aware of how difficult life was for blind Montanans. Surviving life up there really put hair on a person's chest, no matter who you were. She knew all the cards were stacked against any blind person making it in Montana.

Gretch had a story of her own to share just because of all the bullshit she had gone through up there in the flyover zone. She only narrowly managed to turn it all around in her favor . . .

Up there life and death were determined according to a sick and twisted "survival of the fittest" mentality. When Gretchen suddenly wound up blind and brain-injured at the age of twelve, everyone— including her own mother—counted her out of the game of life as a result. She had to fight vehemently to survive and regain her humanity.

Then those. . . you guessed it -- effing lawyers -- tried to do away with her. They wanted to get her out of the way so they could keep her money all for themselves . . .

It took her fifteen years to escape from their trap. It was an uphill battle all the way . . . They even tricked her mother into turning against her.

She learned how to predict her enemies' moves so she could beat them at their own game.

That's how Gretchen became this invincible creature she is today known as "The Measuring Life."

And they think they have a chance of beating her? That's a good one. She's been outsmarting them for decades now . . .

Just by believing in herself . . .

They can't blame Gretchen. She was only responding to what they did to her when she was only twelve years old. She was just minding her own business when those lawyers fucked with her. They stole fifteen years of her life. What was Gretch supposed to do? Now, she would make them pay.

CHAPTER 7

Gretchen remembered the day she established her own legal precedent in that chilly courtroom in Missoula County. It was January 25th, 2012, a. d. It was the day she demanded the state of Montana recognize that she was a human being, created by God and entitled to all the same rights and protections guaranteed to all Americans by the Constitution of the United States of America.

Gretchen was sick of the abuse from this broken legal system.

The judge agreed with her that day and finally set her free.

That was just the beginning though . . .

Ever since that day Gretch had been consumed by this overwhelming need to get revenge on all of them; the lawyers, the neuropsychologists, and her parents.

Proving that they lied. Proving that they needlessly stole fifteen years of her life. She was willing to spend the rest of her days getting revenge on them if it took that long. She would make them pay, one way or another for what they did to her . . .

She never grew weary of researching, reading, writing and speaking out about what they did to her and her family when she was just a little girl.

They all had to sleep. Gretchen never stopped thinking about and scheming her next attacks against those lazy lawyers—especially in her dreams.

It was such an exhilarating experience, living out one's dreams every single day. It really felt like she was making things happen in her own life.

All she had to do was imagine what she wanted to happen next and—ta-da! It would happen. All Gretch could figure was that she had finally gotten her life connected to God's plan for it. Why else was she always finding success in everything she did these days? And this with very little effort from Gretchen.

All she had to do was believe in herself. Was this the glorious gift God had promised? He had always hinted at a great future; if she would only be faithful and keep trying to overcome all the bullshit. Was this really the fulfillment of His promises, right here on earth?

It sure felt and looked like it to Gretch. She was regaining more quality of life in all areas every single day as she worked to rebuild her being.

Did she really have a chance of enjoying a wonderful, healthy life after all she had been through?

So, through all of that, she was making her body and mind strong again. While they were all so busy protecting the damn money, Gretch was busy rebuilding her temple so she could live in it again one day. And here she was—ta-da!

Maybe that's how she finally got the jump on them? Maybe she really did outthink a bunch of stupid lawyers . . . Or was it just dumb luck?

She had an amazing level of energy these days; she was perfectly suited for this assignment. She had managed to turn her body into a virtual machine. Her mind was like a steel trap that was focused like a terminator with her sights set on those feeble-minded lawyers . . .

She would soon figure out how to make them pay; she could feel it. She had been faithful for so many years . . . She loved her little guerrilla war she was fighting against them. They never bothered to acknowledge her declaration of war or her many battles won against them—both in the courtroom and outside of it. She had been taking potshots at them from behind the scenes for decades . . . While they were robbing her blind and keeping her locked away from the world . . . Just how had she escaped again? It was because they all underestimated her.

Oh, to be a fly on their walls today!

She knew they must be scratching their heads even now. How had she done it? How had she managed to walk out of that hospital room in 1989? How had she survived all the years of neglect and abuse that followed?

She kept a lookout for their trap for years. When they finally sprang it in1997, she got caught.

That night they railroaded her into that godforsaken guardianship . . . She knew she had fallen into their trap.

She fought desperately to escape. She finally succeeded.

How had she finally managed to flip the tables on them in that court of law in 2012?

Wasn't she just a brain-injured, blind retard like they said? How had she done it?

The whole world was set against her . . . She just couldn't accept that her life was over. She was just twelve years old when it happened . . . They actually expected her to just say, okay, you guys are right. I give up. Take my liberties away from me.

It was those despicable lawyers who messed it all up. They convinced her mother she was brain dead and should be shut away and not allowed to live life.

She just had to fight back. It was so unfair. She never asked for this fight. Those effing lawyers brought it to her, the night they took her rights away.

All those years Gretchen knew she had youth, intelligence, God and everyone else's mass hysteria and ignorance on her side.

She knew she would one day show them all. She just didn't know when or how much He would help her along the way.

And how had she finally outsmarted all of them? Even Gretch was shocked. That spring day when it all began, she couldn't wrap her newly imploded brain around this mammoth undertaking that God had just forced her into. She was so pissed off at Him. What right did He have? She was a good little girl. She wasn't mean to anyone in or out of school. She helped her mom and dad all the time when she was asked. Why did God choose her?

CHAPTER 8

That evening Gretch and Eddie hung out together at the amateur comedy show. The festivities continued all around them.

Gretch was laughing at the guy up on stage as he told jokes, many of them "blind" jokes. Everyone around them was having a good time.

Gretchen knew learning to laugh at herself had been the first step towards genuine healing.

As the evening passed, Gretch looked around her. The entire area was pumping with energy from the sounds of people having fun. The music and chatter made the whole experience exhilarating.

"Hi there," a sexy, husky male voice said from behind Gretch. She turned around to find a tall, dark and handsome man smiling down at her.

"I knew it was you! I noticed that long, thick, curly auburn hair and those long legs when you first showed up in the lobby earlier this week. My name is Biff Rogers. I'm with the NFB of Nevada," he said as he held his hand out so she could shake it.

Gretch loved the flash of his teeth and his alluring, dark eyes as he smiled down at her. "My name's Gretch. I'm from Arizona. Thank you and your affiliate for hosting this awesome convention. It will surely go down in NFB history," Gretch said, not realizing how prophetic her words were.

As she gave Biff her hand, Gretch hungrily looked this specimen of manliness up and down. Wow! Even Gretchen was impressed with his masculinity.

From the top of his long, white cane to the tips of his Jordans this guy was in tip-top shape and ready to rumble. He was her kind of man— every inch of him.

"I'm from Arizona. I find straight canes a turn-on. Nice to meet you," Gretchen said with a nervous laugh.

Biff gently caressed along the line of her throat with his fingertip as he whispered in her ear, "Wish I could show you what I can do with my cane!"

The suggestive lilt in his voice made the woman inside Gretch clench somewhere deep inside as she relished the carnal feelings his touch and tone elicited from her body.

As the evening wore on Biff and Gretchen pressed closer to one another. Their mutual attraction for each other was evident.

"Would you like to come up to my room for a small party? A few of us NFBers are going to hang out for a while this evening."

"Sure, sounds like fun."

Later as they reclined in Biff's room, Gretch found herself surrounded by several people. They were sitting haphazardly on the floor and furniture in the room, passing the bong around.

"Do you need help lighting it?" Biff whispered in her ear as he handed her the bong.

"No, I've got this!" She expertly wrapped her left hand around the shaft of the bong, balancing the end of it in her right palm. Sliding her hand up the length of the shaft until she felt the bowl against her hand, Gretch set the tip of her left index finger against the edge of the small bowl that contained the ground weed.

Taking the cigarette lighter in her right hand, she flicked it, creating a small flame.

As she held the flame against the ground bud, Gretch pressed her lips into the end of the bong, inhaling deeply. Drawing a big lungful of marijuana smoke from the shaft into the depths of her body, Gretch enjoyed the feeling of sheer ecstasy that overcame all her nerve endings as the natural herb reached her bloodstream.

As she continued her slow, steady sucking on the device, her field of vision began to widen and become clearer.

Gretchen cleared the freshly packed bowl with one, long breath. Biff whistled in admiration.

"Damn, girl! You've got quite a pair of lungs on you. That was amazing."

"I've got skills," Gretch said with a wink.

Later that evening Biff introduced Gretchen to his cane. Gretch shared her skills and knowledge with him as well. Oh, the joys of blind sex! It is a tactile experience!

CHAPTER 9

The next morning after breakfast Gretch and Eddie headed for the exhibit hall to have a look around.

Gretch was enjoying the delicious soreness between her legs as she walked along the carpeted corridor down to the convention center.

Biff was in great shape and had a lot of staying power. He had given her a good work over the night before. She and Biff had shared a lot of themselves with each other during those hours they spent alone. Her mind was filled with flashbacks to the moments filled with sheer ecstasy they had shared together. She felt a dampness between her legs as she thought about it . . . Gretch hoped to bump into Biff again later.

As Gretch and Eddie walked along talking to merchants about what they brought to the convention, Gretchen took her iPhone out of her purse. She logged into her Facebook app. She began a live stream to her Facebook page as she spoke to the merchants about the products they had for sale.

What a fun idea, Gretch thought to herself. This way my friends and family back home can see some of these cool devices.

Maybe someone will learn something helpful from watching my videos . . .

They finally came to the NFB independence market.

"Oh, awesome! I can get a new folding cane right here to replace the one TSA ruined," Gretch said with relief.

After Eddie found a new slate and stylist, they walked up to the cashier together.

"I'd like two of these, please," Gretch said holding out a numbered tag to the woman at the cash register.

"Would you like some cane tips to go along with them? They have tips on them, but they tend to fall off," the woman said.

"Oh, yeah! That's probably a good idea. Can I have four cane tips with the canes, please?"

"The canes are $25 each and the tips are $0.50 each."

Wow, kind of steep but Gretch needed at least one new cane for safety purposes. She never left home without her extra cane.

After sales tax, the total came to just under $60.

Pulling her credit card from her purse she handed it to the woman. After the woman finished processing the order, she offered Gretch a hard surface where she could sign her credit card receipt.

The woman produced a thin piece of plastic. "Let's use this signature guide. It will make your signature more legible."

What a cool little device, Gretch thought as she examined the plastic signature guide. "Can I have one of these as well, please?"

After paying for all her purchases Gretch and Eddie continued along the line of tables.

When they came to the job fair Davis had told her about Gretch was amazed. What a great idea!

Gretch was talking with an international company about doing some work online for them when Eddie excitedly nudged her.

"Guess what I just did?" he hissed in her ear.

"What?" Gretch asked, mildly irritated. She hated being elbowed by people.

"I just spoke to the BEP recruiter about the Business Enterprise Program. It sounds like a great opportunity for someone in my position."

"That's wonderful, Eddie. The opportunity will definitely enhance your family's life. Good for you for taking the initiative to step out and make contact with them."

As Gretch and Eddie continued through the exhibit hall she was amazed at all the information and advocacy available through the NFB. The teacher inside Gretch was overwhelmed with it all.

"Hi again," Gretch heard someone whisper in her ear.

She was almost afraid to believe her ears.

"Biff! What are you doing? It's great to see you," Gretch gushed as Biff swept her into his big, muscular arms.

"Hi baby," he said as he hungrily placed kisses up and down her throat.

"Oh, Biff!" she breathed, overcome with feelings of lust. "Let's hang out in my room tonight, okay?"

"Sure, whatever you want, babe. As long as I can be with you again tonight."

"I'm going to go up to my room and chill out for a bit. I may take a nap. Call me later when you're ready to hang out together," Gretch said to Biff as he walked away.

"Of course. I have staff duty this evening, but I'll come up to your room right after."

When Gretch got up to her room she laid down and closed her eyes for a few minutes. She was awakened by the jingle of her cell phone a few hours later . . .

CHAPTER 10

"Hello?" Gretch said in a groggy voice as she held the noisy device to her ear, wiping the sleep from her eyes.

Wow, she had slept really deep. She must be getting a lot of great exercise here at the convention. (She was concerned when she realized she wouldn't have access to her treadmill for a week.)

"Hi, sissy!" Gretch heard her little sister's voice.

"Hi, Alex. What's up?" Gretch said, gritting her teeth. She hated that nickname Alex insisted on using for her.

"I'm in a Veyo on my way home from my doctor's appointment," Alex said as Gretch half listened.

Gretch had a lot going on here in Vegas. She just hoped her little sister was safe while she was out of town.

"Listen, this driver is the same one that picked us up about a month ago, remember?" Alex asked.

Gretch remembered. She enjoyed riding with Alex to her appointments if only so she could get out of the house away from her computer and meet a new person now and again.

As Alex continued filling in details of the ride in question, Gretch really did recall the encounter with the man. Gretch certainly remembered that day. She climbed in the front seat of his car and introduced herself to the driver; just like she had done so many other times on so many other rides over the decades.

Gretch had always made a real effort to be friendly to people she met. She was practicing her "elevator" pitch that day.

What had possessed her to go that one step further that day? He wasn't the first private driver she'd met who was also a movie director. Why had she confidently held out her hand to him declaring that she was "an . . . author who wrote a book that needed to be made into a movie for the whole world to see?" What possessed her to be so bold?

"He wants to talk to you. I gave him a copy of your book the other day. He said he read it. He wants to talk to you about helping you make your movie."

The driver had taken her seriously.

Well, now that Gretch thought about it, those short sighted lawyers should have taken her more seriously. This was her big chance to show the world just how serious she really was.

"Please give him my number and tell him I'm out of town for a few days. If he gets my voice mail when he calls me, he better just leave me a message. I may not hear my phone here at the convention."

When the call came in later Gretch was all nerves. What does one say to a filmmaker?

"Hello, this is Geno Marx. Can I speak to Gretchen, please?"

"Speaking," Gretch tried to say with professionalism.

Gretch was in shock during the entire phone conversation. She was literally listening to one of God's miracles on the other end of the phone. He had brought her an award-winning movie director to help her make her film!

Talk about confirmation that you've been on the right path all along!

CHAPTER 11

Gretch literally floated through the rest of the convention that week. She couldn't wait to get home and talk to this guy about her movie project.

When Biff knocked on her door that evening Gretch was beside herself with excitement.

Biff went hard and rough that night; just the way Gretch liked it.

"Do you want to sit with me at our table at the banquet?" Biff asked as they enjoyed some pillow talk after a particularly intense lovemaking session.

"I'd love to. Thanks for asking me," she said, squeezing Biff's shoulders affectionately as she came in close to him for another long, passionate lip-lock. "I've always felt like a loner in the NFB. I feel comfortable in all of the affiliates."

Gretch and Biff continued meeting for fabulous sexcapades during the remaining few days of the convention.

The night of the banquet Biff and Gretchen were enjoying each other's company as they sat together.

Gretch was listening to the keynote speaker while she ate her side salad. Damn croutons! She thought to herself as the hard little bit of bread shot off her saucer and across the room. Did anyone notice? Thank God this was a blind convention!

Later, Gretch found herself struggling to stay awake as they listened to the national president of the NFB bloviating. She lifted her head sleepily up from the table, rubbing her eyes in an effort to stay awake.

Biff stayed with Gretch that night. They couldn't keep their hands off each other.

The morning she was supposed to check out of the hotel Gretch overslept. She didn't hear the seven a.m. wake-up call she scheduled with the front desk the night before.

Gretch was awakened by a loud knocking on her room door.

"Yes?" Gretch said groggily through the crack in her hotel room door a few minutes later.

"We need to get in to clean your room," a voice said in broken English.

"Oh, shit! I overslept," Gretch exclaimed as she ran around the room, grabbing up her possessions and stuffing them into her suitcase.

She stuck her nose in her armpit to see how bad she smelled. Could she skip her shower if she drenched herself in perfume?

She just took a shower a few hours ago when she got back to her room after another rousing sex match with Biff. Fuck; she loved black men!

She ran her fingers through her hair to see how greasy it was. If she brushed it really good and kept it up off her neck so she didn't sweat today she just might be okay until she got home this evening.

CHAPTER 12

It was a few days after Gretchen established her company Blue Butterfly Enterprises in August 2019 that she was on Facebook.

As she scrolled through her newsfeed her JAWS suddenly shrieked: "Let Us Play Us!"

What was this?

Gretch took a closer look at the post.

It was a post from the National Federation of the Blind. The federation was promoting their new drive to persuade filmmakers to cast blind actors and actresses in blind roles in movies and television.

Gretch loved the NFB. Sometimes they just didn't go far enough in her book.

Why stop at blind people playing blind roles in movies? Why can't a blind actor or actress play sighted roles just as well? It was all just acting, right?

This caused Gretchen to look at her newly formed company with a mind and heart that were committed to equal opportunity for anyone who wanted to participate in her projects. Gretchen used her own knowledge learned from years of having to build her own accessibility to put her company together. She knew she could make virtually anything in life accessible if she just thought about it long enough.

Gretchen found great success in building all facets of her company while staying committed to these important diversity standards.

The events that occurred over the next two years just confirmed for Gretchen all the more that God really had His hand on her life. He really did have a good reason for what He allowed to happen to her when she was that little girl up in North-Central Montana . . . She hadn't been alone after all.

AFTERWORD

It was about six months after the birth of **BBE** when Gretch was sitting out on her veranda one evening.

She looked up when she heard a loud disturbance nearby.

She gasped when something whooshed past her head in the darkness.

Gretch squinted as she caught movement in the air in front of her. She caught a glimpse of a Chinese bat as it flew past her face.

Gretch hated bats. She smiled when she saw a giant, beautiful, blue butterfly as it came up behind the ugly little bat.

Gretch watched in fascination as the bat tried in vain to avoid the giant blue butterfly.

The butterfly wrapped its many legs around the struggling bat, ripping its ugly little head off before letting its twitching carcass drop to the ground.

MY PREMONITION

CHAPTER 1

That final school year; the one just before the accident—I was twelve years old. I was maturing from a little girl into a young lady. I thought I knew where I was going in life.

I had always been a God follower. I always had a desire to please Him and seek His will for my life; no matter what it was.

I was seeking direction in my life as I prepared to move from elementary into junior high and beyond.

Whenever I talked to God about these concerns, He kept showing me images of Mother Teresa in my mind; as if He were trying to tell me something.

I wasn't raised Catholic, but I knew who Mother Teresa was. I thought I had some inkling of the magnitude of what she had sacrificed for Him when called upon.

This is why I wasn't particularly surprised when I awoke from that coma to find myself in that broken, shattered condition. Rebuilding myself would clearly be a lifelong project.

I was royally pissed off at God though. I knew He was responsible from the very beginning.

Imagine how I scoffed at Him when He insisted that I should just calm down and trust Him?

As I cried out to Him in anger and bitterness; I literally felt Him as He consoled me.

Was this real?

I realized I had no other choice than to go with it. I literally had to put God to the test. Were all those old stories from the Old and New Testaments true . . . or weren't they? I intended to find out.

CHAPTER 2

I didn't recall being consulted on this beforehand. Were those random images of that nun God's idea of a sign? (Give me a break!)

How could He just expect me to sacrifice the rest of my life to be an example for others?

But the truth was; I did remember. I remembered when He would pop an image of that nun into my head; every time I let my heart wander away to wonder what He might have planned for my future. The fact I wasn't a practicing Catholic just made this entire experience so much more poignant for me.

These were the thoughts I was having in the months leading up to the "accident."

Imagine how this helped to solidify my faith in Him in the coming months and years as I argued on my behalf in the face of all those medical and legal professionals? I tried to tell them all; the doctors, lawyers and even my own mother what was actually going on. But they were all suddenly struck blind. They just couldn't see what God and I were working on.

These early experiences really gave me a strong faith in God when I needed it most. Imagine knowing the outcome before you even get started on a battle like this one?

CHAPTER 3

Learning to live according to God's timeline was the hardest part for me. I have always been extremely impatient (just ask anyone who knows me).

I take God literally wherever possible in His Word. He clearly said: ". . . a day will be as a thousand years and a thousand years will be as a day."

In my mind this can only mean one thing; God is in charge of all eternity. I realized I had to change my perspective to match His if I were going to get on His timeline.

I had to understand that He works on really big projects; on projects that take a long time from our narrow, human perspective. These projects take just a glimmer of time on His cosmic calendar.

When He created us; He made us to be eternal creatures. That leaves a lot of time for Him to mold us the way He wants us. He is building each of us to be very complex creatures.

Don't allow yourself to put God in a box. He can get a lot accomplished in a short time if you hand Him the keys to the car of your life and let Him drive.

This faith has served me well my life long; just read my books if you don't believe me!

I had to focus on my faith regarding His timeline so much more when those stupid lawyers and my parents locked me under that guardianship. It was obvious they intended to keep me locked away for the rest of this life. Imagine what that was like?

I literally spent fifteen years fighting to get out of their trap.

I saw red the day I finally walked out of court a free woman. I've been busy taking back my life ever since; and I don't care who doesn't like it. I have earned the right to live my life for myself. And, oh boy, am I living it!

Eat my dust; is all I have to say to those stupid doctors, lawyers and my parents. They haven't seen anything yet.

It has taken a long time for me to forgive my parents . . . I haven't bothered to try forgiving the doctors and the rest of them. They're not worth the time it would take me to focus on forgiving them. I'm getting even instead. Happy reading, guys!

Today, I realize those fifteen years were but a blip of time on the calendar of eternity. I have many more days left before me.

I managed to take what I learned all those years and, using God's power, magnify it to help me recover in leaps and bounds.

Viewing all the obstacles in my life through this prism filled with His power has enabled me to achieve whatever I want in life. It has helped me to hyper-magnify all my results in life.

Don't believe me? Just read my books. In them, I share many of the miracles God has performed in my life.

The strange thing is, my faith looks completely different from that of anyone else I know. I have truly "personalized" my faith.

In a huge way, I feel like I was eons ahead of those "educated" people I was dealing with all those years ago.

I wish I could hand them each a copy of all my books today. It is their blurry faces and ignorant voices I see and hear in my mind as I write every word of my books.

It's okay if they don't wind up reading my books though. I'm actually making a movie; for their viewing pleasure! (See what I mean by the way He magnifies all my efforts in life?) Have you ever met a legally blind movie producer? (Only in God's world—lol!)

CHAPTER 4

How did I start manifesting all these miracles in my life though?

First came faith. I studied my personal beliefs and everything I had ever been taught in church, school and throughout my community.

That's where I found the faith I needed.

Faith in God.

Faith in my country.

And faith in myself.

I combined this faith with action. I made a bet. I told those doctors and the rest of them in no uncertain terms that this fight wasn't over. In fact, I was only getting started. So, I went to work. I had a lot of work to do. I had to get my quality of life back—somehow.

None of them believed me. In reality, they all cast their lots against me. Many of them actually flung large stumbling blocks into my path. The doctors. The lawyers. My teachers.

Eventually, even my own mother.

It was just God and me. Holding out. Against them all.

That was over thirty years ago.

And I won. I proved all the "experts" wrong. God and me.

I won because I was obedient to Him when the chips were down. I cast my lot with God.

When they said there was just no way, I reminded them, but God. For years, I kept saying: "But God." And He heard me, even if they didn't.

He blessed my faithfulness.

I started pointing out to people every little miracle I saw God doing in my life. And the miracles started getting bigger. And more frequent. Until I was seeing larger miracles in my life every single day. And I kept telling people. And they were seeing the miracles for themselves. Until it was over. They lost and I won!

I got so far ahead of that stupid brain injury that none of them could catch me anymore. He blessed my obedience. That's all that happened; I think. He was good on His word. I was obedient when He asked me to be. I sacrificed years of my life being obedient in this way. I just had to learn to see things from His perspective, not mine.

What about you? You too can empower yourself today by changing your own perspective. Only you have the power. Remember, God put it right inside of you when He first created you. No one can take that power from you . . . unless you let them.

They tried to take my power from me. A long time ago. I knew better though. I still have my power today. And it's getting bigger every single day.

I thought this fight I just described would be the most important fight of my life . . . I was wrong.

CHAPTER 5

I grew up hearing rumors of the "Shadow Government." Where I come from, people have always predicted that there were people of ill intent lurking in our government; just waiting for their opportunity to usher in Communism. These rumors terrified me as a child.

Today, as we all watch this unfolding right in front of us, I'm just royally pissed off. If these democrats and the rest of these anti-American politicians and elites think they are going to get away with this, they have another thing coming.

Today, I feel like a cowboy who spent the last thirty-plus years riding a bucking bronco.

In Biblical terms; I've been wrestling with God.

Now, for all my less informed readers let me point something out to you. Jacob also wrestled with God. It's not a crime. And it builds character.

Just as those doctors and lawyers underestimated me; these shysters who are trying to overthrow our government and take away our way of life have underestimated the spirit of the American people. President Donald Trump awakened this spirit in us all and they will never snuff out this flame. The flame of freedom. It now burns in the hearts of all Americans. How can they possibly stop us all from living our lives to the fullest? Don't allow them to stop you and yours.

—The Measuring Life

AFTERWORD

The American people will surely prevail. I'm as certain of this as I was that I would win in my own battle. I dare all of you to put Him to the test today.

ABOUT THE AUTHOR

Rebecca Meadows is an author, blogger, life coach, motivational speaker, founder of Blue Butterfly Enterprises LLC, host of Becca's World on YouTube and an executive movie producer.

Becca lives in Mesa Arizona with her family; where she leads her company.

Becca is the author of "Because You're Blind"

"Changing My Perspective"

And the short story collection "Metamorphosis."

Becca is well on her way to completing production of her first full-length movie. Meanwhile she is working on finishing her fourth book; "Still Busy Steering."

You can email Becca directly at info@bluebutterflyenterprises.com. And follow her on her YouTube channel Becca's World.

Through videos on her YouTube channel, her writings and her movie projects; Ms. Meadows is fulfilling the purpose for which she was created, m- to educate the world.

Ms. Meadows spends her days working hard on several projects; each designed to help others discover the power they possess to change their own lives.

Rebecca leads a very inspired life. She invites you to walk with her today.

OTHER BOOKS
BY REBECCA S. MEADOWS

Because You're Blind

Changing My Perspective

(Coming Soon) Still Busy Steering

Please visit bluebutterflyenterprises.com
and check out Becca's World on
YouTube to get more information.

Made in the USA
Columbia, SC
14 March 2024

32819217R00111